ABOUT THE AUTHOR

James Warden was a teacher for forty years and retired in 2006. He now enjoys his retirement as much as he enjoyed his time in the education service and is catching up on those things which he left undone and ought to have done – in particular, his writing. He writes every morning between nine o'clock and noon, for thirty-six weeks of the year.

He is fortunate enough to be able to act in several Norwich theatres – the Maddermarket, the Sewell Barn and, with the Great Hall Players, at the Assembly House – and this experience informs his writing. His stage adaptation of Laurie Lee's *As I Walked Out One Midsummer Morning* was performed at the Sewell Barn Theatre in November 2009. His original play, *Letters from a Boy in the Trenches*, which was based on the letters of a WW1 soldier, was performed in Marchington, Staffordshire in 2015.

James is married – for the second time – and lives in Norfolk. He and his wife travel as much as possible. They have visited Italy (where they were married in 2002) several times, Canada, Bermuda, Egypt, India, the Czech Republic, New England, Poland, Slovenia, Antarctica, the Falkland Islands, Alaska, the Galapagos Islands, Australia and Switzerland. In 2018, they travelled across the USA on Route 66. They have also taken several holidays in various Mediterranean resorts – the basis for his first novel, *Three Women of a Certain Age*, which was published in July 2010, and *Bingham Goes to Cannes*, to be published in 2024.

During his years in education, he wrote about twenty play scripts for children. These included the one that formed the basis for his children's story, *The Great Gobbler and his Home Baking Factory at the North Pole*, which he wrote in 1982 and published in December 2010.

He has three sons by his first marriage, and they inspired two of his novels – *The Vampire's Homecoming*, which was published in 2011, and *The One-eyed Dwarf*, published in 2012. With them and his first wife, he also travelled to the southern states of North America, France, Germany (West and East), Estonia and what was Czechoslovakia.

WRITING BY JAMES WARDEN

Letters from a Boy in the Trenches
*(Adapted from the letters home of Sydney Harrison
and performed by the Marchington Amateur
Dramatic Society in November 2015.)*

BINGHAM SEEKS AN ODD COUPLE

BY

JAMES WARDEN

Grosvenor House
Publishing Limited

This book is published by
Grosvenor House Publishing Ltd
Link House
140 The Broadway, Tolworth, Surrey, KT6 7HT.
www.grosvenorhousepublishing.co.uk

This book is a work of fiction. Any resemblance to
people or events, past or present, is purely coincidental.

A CIP record for this book
is available from the British Library

ISBN 978-1-83975-357-2

Chapter One
LOCKED IN EACH OTHER'S ARMS

If Bingham's daughter, Fiorenza, had not come up to Suffolk for the weekend he would never have heard of the odd couple; but over dinner on the Friday evening their story and his search began.

Fiorenza was one of 'the twins', as people would often refer to them; she and her sister, Cecilia, were Lina and Bingham's second and third children, and Lina had named them after two of her favourite opera singers. She'd closed the door on her own career when she married Bingham in her mid-thirties. Looking at her daughter across the dining room table, Lina was reminded of herself at that age: strong faced with large dark eyes, a full mouth and a nose rather too long, she'd always felt, and a mass of thick, curly hair. Nevertheless, it was the face that brought her roles as strong or passionate women in the world of opera: Elizabeth the First in *Maria Stuarda*, Donna Elvira in *Don Giovanni* to name but two.

It was after the meal as they sat at the table talking that Fiorenza, who was a researcher for the BBC, mentioned the incident on the Costa del Sol.

"I heard the story from a friend of mine – a Spanish journalist. It made Sky News and some national papers in this country but then vanished into the usual obscurity of such stories once the sensational element had faded.

It appears that the couple had moved to Spain when they retired. They had a villa – as these properties are called, but are quite small really – in the hills behind a coastal resort called Guaro del Mar. They were 'odd' in as much as they never came home even to see their grandchildren: they seemed quite content in each other's company. Evidently, they were devoted to each other – "always locked in each other's arms", as one of their children said to the newspapers. They were in their seventies – rather like you two!"

"Excuse me," interrupted Lina, "Your father might be in his seventies, but I'm holding on to the sixties for a little while longer."

"All right, Mum – let's say they were well retired! To go on! They were expecting friends round for an evening meal – people they'd met since going to Spain: other English couples and some locals. When the guests arrived at the villa there was no one to be seen. The place was completely empty. But – and this is what captured the imagination of the headline writers – a meal had been prepared. Various salads were waiting in the kitchen and a rabbit casserole was simmering on the stove.

Their friends waited for half an hour or so and then phoned home to England, knowing the couple had family here, but the children said they knew nothing. They said that Colin and Patty always phoned home on the Sunday evening at 6 o'clock and that they were surprised not to have received a call because the couple were religious in doing so."

"And this was the Sunday evening?" asked Bingham.

"Yes, Dad."

"Go on."

"The Guardia Civil were called in and began an investigation but nothing seemed amiss: there were no signs of a break-in, the couple had no criminal record and they were well-liked in the little town where they shopped. One local said that "they had not been doing anything strange".

"Why should they have been doing anything strange? It seems an odd comment … Did your journalist friend pick it up at the time? … I thought the Spanish ate later in the evening?"

"They're English, Bing, and elderly," said Lina, "I think it highly likely that they ate their evening meal at the same time as us. We never enjoy a heavy meal at nine o'clock do we?"

"No, I suppose we don't. How long would a rabbit casserole take to cook, Lina?"

"It depends on how many people you were entertaining."

"For the sake of argument, let's suppose they were expecting four guests."

"Well, let me think. They would have sautéed the rabbit first together with the onions, garlic, chilli and whatever else they were including … I suppose, once the stock was added, the stewing process would have taken about an hour – possibly less."

"So, the couple would have disappeared within the space of an hour somewhere around six o'clock in the evening?"

"The lady would have had the casserole on the go before she planned to make the phone call. I think you could pinpoint the time they disappeared at somewhere between a quarter to six and a quarter past, depending upon how far the casserole was from being ready when the guests arrived."

"Listening to you two is like wandering into a parallel universe," Fiorenza remarked, watching her parents, and smiling.

"Come and have a look at the bees," said Bingham.

It was not often his daughter came home nowadays and Bingham enjoyed being alone with her when she did, wandering pathways they had walked or run when she was a child. They were easy in each other's company and he didn't feel the need to speak unduly. Bingham half-listened: he took in what Fiorenza said but rarely commented. It was simply a pleasure to hear her voice.

When they reached the orchard, he showed her the hives she'd helped him with as a child, and they watched the last bees returning at the end of a day's foraging. He explained that the workers had been busy already, replenishing their winter stores from the spring blossom: blackthorn, forsythia, the willow by the pond, primroses and dandelions.

By the time they returned, Lina had cleared the table, filled the dishwasher and was brewing coffee.

"Go into the sitting room," she said, "I'll bring this through in a minute."

"Funnily enough, your mum and I have often talked of living abroad," said Bingham, returning to a thought he'd had earlier in the evening.

"You mean you'd leave Bob's Farm!"

"Probably not, but we feel the cold now we're older and living in a warmer climate has its attractions."

Bingham caught Lina's eye as he spoke and realized the same thought was passing through her mind

It was later in the evening, after Fiorenza had retired and Bingham had given the dogs their last walk of the day, when Lina returned to her daughter's story.

"You were thinking about how our children would feel if we simply disappeared in a foreign country weren't you, Bing?"

"Yes."

"Why don't you have a nose around? Take Brockie with you. Aren't there plenty of golf courses in that part of Spain?"

"I hate golf."

"The thought of a round with you might persuade him to come. An ex-policeman would prove useful, I imagine."

"Are you trying to get rid of me?"

"No, but I feel the same as you do. I'd hate to think that we might just disappear from the face of the Earth in our seventies. Putting aside the possibility of an alien abduction there doesn't seem to be many possible answers, does there?"

"That's what I thought, Lina. It all hangs on that missing half an hour. I'll give Brockie a ring in the morning."

Ex-Detective Chief Inspector Simon Brockie was only too pleased to get away from his wife, Aileen, for a few days: she was one of those women who expected her husband to be on call when needed and his retirement was proving to be less joyful than he'd anticipated.

He was not keen, however, on Bingham's reason for going to the Costa del Sol, believing that police work should be left to the professionals "even if they're foreigners". Bingham smiled and promised he'd "try not to win at golf", an occurrence not likely to happen but a comment that made Brockie realise why he liked Bingham's company: self-mockery is always attractive.

Lina had booked their flights, their hotel and arranged a taxi from Malaga airport to Guaro del Mar, a distance of just over forty miles. It was still early spring; the air was limpid and the sky an almost transparent blue. Even in the air-conditioned taxi, listening to the driver's travelogue, Bingham could smell the sea.

So excited was he that they dropped off their bags immediately on checking into the La Fonda and made their way to the quay. Before the advent of tourism, Guaro had relied entirely on its fishing boats and these still adorned the small harbour, painted in bright blues and reds and yellows between bands of brilliant white. White never seemed quite so intense at home, thought Bingham, watching the fishermen at work. He noted the small cruisers and a few yachts moored alongside the new marina, jostling for space in the small harbour, and he wondered who would win the struggle.

He and Brockie strolled along the quayside beyond the harbour entrance and saw the stretches of golden sand now claimed by the hotels that had sprung up along the coast to cope with the invasion of the English. They stopped off for a beer at one of the many cafes and Bingham began to feel the sense of isolation that always dropped in on him when he was abroad: a sense that nothing was real, that he was living in a vacuum of sun and leisure. Perhaps that was what had attracted Colin and Patty Mayhew to the Costa and the little villa in the hills where they had found peace in their retirement and from where they disappeared.

Back at the La Fonda, Bingham asked directions to the odd couple's villa, quoting the address Fiorenza had obtained from her journalist friend and emailed to her father. His query was met with raised eyebrows and an obvious reluctance on the part of the receptionist to talk. It was only when Brockie, bringing his bulk to bear on the question, leaned over the counter that the young woman suggested they should ask a taxi driver.

The man smiled, removed a cigarette from between a set of jagged white teeth, and chuckled to himself. He took Bingham and Brockie to the corner of the street adjacent to the hotel and waved his free arm in the direction of the hill that backed the town.

"Mire. Siga derecho por esta carretera."

"Esta lejos?"

"No, a diez minutos andando"

The two friends made their way uphill between squares of closely packed houses, Bingham asking Brockie whether he had ever known a taxi driver turn down a fare when it involved a ten-minute walk.

It was, however, a pleasant stroll. They passed beneath balconies overhung with flowers and from which washing was strung across the street, one balcony to the other; and, once again that morning, Bingham was reminded how pleasant it was to live where the sun shone and the breeze from the sea was warm.

The sounds of women's voices imbued the air with a sense of purpose; here, normal people lived their lives doing everyday things. It was late morning and the smell of cooking was everywhere: fish, cloves and peppers, ripe tomatoes, black pepper and parsley.

The road turned out of the main town and soon artificially landscaped housing appeared, built for the English settlers who came to live out their days in a foreign land, the sun on their backs, the taste of hefty red wine on their palates, the sweet smell of fish steaks in tomato sauce in their noses.

The Mayhew's villa, a small one but with its own pool, was bordered by various acacia plants around a small lawn that wound its way down from the house to the road. Among the shrubs, a young man stood with a hoe in his hand and a puzzled expression on his face. When Bingham spoke to him, he looked down at the ground and resumed his weeding.

"Do you speak English?"

The young man shook his head and so Bingham continued in Spanish much to the gardener's surprise. It took some time, but Bingham established that his name was Betran Julio and that he and his wife, Camila, were employed to look after the villas. Eventually, Bingham asked:

"Is this the villa of Senor and Senora Mayhew?"

"Si."

"Did you know them?"

"Si."

Both acknowledgements were uttered in a subdued voice and the young man's eyes remained fixed firmly on the ground.

"Had you seen them the day they disappeared?"

The young man's discomfort was now so apparent it became almost hostile; his 'si' was replaced with a grunt and a glance over his shoulder towards the road.

"I have come from England. Senor and Senora Mayhew's children are worried about them. They have not heard from them since the day they disappeared … They have sons and daughters, you see, and grandchildren. Can you tell me what you know of Senor and Senora Mayhew?"

The mention of family seemed to mellow the young man. He placed his hoe against one of the spiky bushes and gestured that Bingham and Brockie should follow him onto the terrace behind which patio doors opened into the main living room of the Mayhew's villa.

"What were they like – Senor and Senora Mayhew?"

"They were good people – nice people."

"They treated you well?"

"Yes – a drink on hot days ... They would invite me to sit with them and rest."

"Did they ever go out? What were their interests?"

"Senor Mayhew had a small boat – a cruiser – but Senora Mayhew did not like the water. She was afraid. Sometimes they would go down to the quay and sit on the boat and have some coffee."

"Senor Mayhew would go out alone?"

"Yes – sometimes. Sometimes one of their friends would visit and then Senor Mayhew would go with the man while the lady stayed and talked with the Senora."

"They would go boating – Senor Mayhew and his friend?"

"Yes."

"Where did Senor Mayhew and his wife go together?"

"To the shops. Sometimes they would walk along the quayside in the morning. Sometimes they would go down to the beach."

"The car in the driveway – is that the Senor's?"

"Yes."

"Did they ever drive out together?"

"Sometimes, when the weather was cool."

"For the day?"

"Sometimes. Sometimes they would be back for the siesta. Sometimes with friends. Sometimes alone."

"How far did they go?"

Betran Julio shrugged.

"To the hills, maybe. Once a week Senor Mayhew would go alone to Malaga – otherwise they were always together."

"Locked in each other's arms?"

Betran frowned at the phrase and then smiled.

"They were very much in love," he said.

"So, we understand … Do you have a key to the house?"

Again, Betran frowned, but this time with disapproval rather than puzzlement.

"No. My wife, Camila, cleans. She has a key."

"Senor and Senora Mayhew did not keep a key under a flowerpot?"

"It is possible."

"So that you could fetch yourself a drink if you were thirsty?"

"Si."

"May we see round the house?"

"I cannot."

"Of course. I understand."

During Bingham's conversation with Betran, Simon Brockie, who understood not a word of what was being said, had walked around the house. When he returned, he had a key in his hand.

"People never learn," he said, "it's always under a flowerpot somewhere, usually by the front or back door. We shouldn't be doing this, George, but I'd just like a quick glimpse at the kitchen."

He let himself in through the patio doors, while Bingham sat on one of the white, steel chairs to rest his feet. He smiled at Betran, whose worried expression had intensified when Brockie entered the house.

"It's all right. My friend's a policeman," said Bingham, unsure why he had made the remark, but supposing it was to reassure the young gardener who looked anything but comforted. "Do you know which of their friends were coming for a meal on the evening they disappeared?"

"Yes. My wife, Camila, was the one who bought the rabbit for Senora Mayhew. She has ... contacts on the market."

"Senor Mayhew did not hunt?"

"No."

"There is no gun in the house?"

"I do not know."

Bingham was aware that his questions were the result of his scattered thoughts rather than a planned interrogation. He'd felt this when searching for Natalie Beddoes, and thought that Brockie, as a professional policeman, would have obtained more information had he only spoken Spanish.

"The friends who came – who were they?"

"English people from the houses," replied Betran, waving one hand around the dwellings clustered on the hillside, "And Senor Higuera and his wife from the town."

"Would they have walked here?"

"Si."

Bingham looked down the road he and Brockie had followed from the village. It seemed to be the only way to reach the Mayhew's house, coming and going. He had, at least, discovered two things about such investigations: time was of the essence, time and who was where at that moment.

As he pondered, Brockie came out onto the patio shaking his head.

"Nothing. Clean as a whistle."

Bingham caught the smile on Betran's face.

"Your wife tidied up?"

"Si."

"And you speak a little English?"

The young man smiled.

"I speak a little – not much."

"They all speak a little. They have to, to get by."

The speaker was a man Bingham judged to be in his sixties. He stood in the roadway, slightly out of sight, hidden by one of the larger acacias, and Bingham wondered how long he'd been listening to their conversation. Watching Betran's face, Bingham noted that the young man seemed put out rather than perturbed.

"I'm Fred Jackson. I've got a boat in the harbour."

He walked onto the patio and stretched out his hand in greeting. Both Bingham and Brockie accepted the gesture of friendship. Fred Jackson was one of those men described as grizzled, whether because he couldn't be bothered to wash and shave when abroad or because he wanted to create an impression: the look of an old 'sea dog' – a phrase Bingham remembered from stories he'd read as a boy. In those stories such men could always be trusted and relied upon to supply the last piece of information that completed the puzzle, clicking all else into place.

"Did you know the Mayhews?"

"Yes. Patty wasn't keen on the water. I used to go out with Colin."

"How often?" asked Brockie.

Fred Jackson looked at Brockie before he answered, and Bingham noticed a certain expression in the man's face. He, too, had been surprised by the tone of the question: it was one that impelled an answer.

"Perhaps once a week, perhaps more often."

"Where did you go?"

"Along the coast."

"To do what?"

"It's a pleasant trip and we usually took our fishing rods. It was a nice day out. It got us away from the wives."

"Did you catch much?"

"Always, and when we got back, we'd share the catch or sometimes have a meal together. My wife enjoys cooking and so did Patty. Marmitako was my wife's speciality and Colin loved it."

"Fish stew?" asked Bingham. "Is your wife Spanish?"

"That's right. We have a place in the town. I've lived here for years. I love it."

During the conversation, Betran had returned to his gardening, hoeing carefully between the shrubs, watching the ground.

"You're keeping an eye on the Mayhew's place while they're away, are you?" suggested Brockie.

"That's right."

"Then perhaps you'd better take care of this. I found it under the flowerpot. It's a temptation for burglars and the house is well furnished."

"Yes, thanks. That's a good idea."

"What do you think has happened to Colin and Patty?" asked Bingham.

"We don't know. It's a surprise to us all. No one has any idea … Look, I'd best be going. It's almost time for our siesta and I don't want to disappoint the wife."

Fred Jackson laughed, smiled at Bingham and cast a last look at Brockie before setting off down the hill. When he'd gone Brockie called out to Betran.

"Is he often here?"

"No," replied the young man.

"I thought not," said Brockie quietly to Bingham, "otherwise he'd have known about and removed the key. I wonder who sent him to find out what we were after – the receptionist or the taxi driver. I don't like being lied to, George, and if Fred Jackson wasn't actually lying, he was being evasive, which to me is much the same thing. Besides, I've seen him somewhere before – back home in the old days. I'll make a few enquiries. I'm glad you asked me to come. It's a bit like old times."

Bingham walked over to Betran Julio, shook his hand and thanked him for his help. Brockie followed suit and then he and Bingham walked back into town looking forward to a long lunch break, Bingham wondering whether marmitako might be on the menu. During his time in Spain as a young man he had enjoyed similar dishes in seaside towns many times: the memory of tuna balanced by sweet peppers and cider and topped with potatoes assailed his palate.

Chapter Two

CHANCE TAKES A HAND

They decided to eat at a little café on the waterfront rather than back at their hotel and so it was almost three o'clock before they returned ready to unpack their clothes and make themselves known.

They had spoken little during the meal, both occupied with their own thoughts, and it was only after the honey-baked figs with ice cream and hazelnuts had been cleared away that Brockie said:

"I hope we haven't bitten off more than we can chew here, George."

Bingham smiled at the connection he thought he detected in his friend's train of thought and asked what he meant.

"The Costa del Sol is renowned, as no doubt you know, for harbouring the low life of the British criminal world. Once I've identified our grizzled friend, I might be able to tell you more."

At the hotel, Jorge Demara, Fiorenza's journalist friend, was waiting for them. Looking at the tall, lean, sun-tanned young man, Bingham hoped his daughter didn't know him too well: that the relationship was a distant, professional one.

"Mr Bingham? Fiorenza said you were coming, but to be honest I don't see that there's much you can do. The local authorities have investigated the disappearance of the Mayhews thoroughly and found nothing."

Bingham ignored the misconception inherent in the words and introduced Simon Brockie, who Jorge Demara eyed from head to foot.

"Are you a policeman?"

"Retired."

As Bingham admired his acuteness, the Spaniard's manner became disconcerted. He shuffled from foot to foot and rubbed his fingers down an immaculately tailored, linen suit.

"Can I get you a drink?"

Bingham disliked hotel lounges intensely: everything was too new, too marshalled, too polished, and always someone hovered, waiting to ask if anything was required. All Bingham really wanted was to unpack and feel he'd arrived.

"That will be most welcome," said Brockie, and the three of them found themselves sitting by a spotless glass window overlooking a large blue pool, sharing a bottle of light, red wine that Bingham thought was similar to a Beaujolais, one of his favourites.

Jorge Demara seemed unable to start the conversation. Bingham was content to watch him, wondering whether in his concern for his daughter's well-being he had misjudged the young man. After all, his daughter's wild nature wasn't the fault of any young man, and Bingham's almost automatic distrust of handsome foreigners was probably unfair. Nevertheless, she would have been unduly attracted to this man's lean physique that was matched by a natural tan, a mop of thick black hair and a pair of eyes that no doubt sparkled in female company.

"What can you tell us about the criminal fraternity in Guaro?" asked Brockie.

"It keeps itself to itself, rather like the Mafia in the States. If you don't interfere with them, they have no reason to show an interest in you. People go about their everyday lives much as they do anywhere else in the world."

"Have you come across a man who calls himself Fred Jackson?"

"No."

"He appeared at the Mayhew's today not long after we arrived … "

"You've been to the Mayhew's villa!"

"Yes. Mr Jackson seemed evasive."

"About what?"

"He told us he was keeping an eye on the Mayhew's villa because he and they were friends, but he hadn't been there a great deal and we found a key under a flowerpot – something I hope someone caring for my house would have removed to avoid a burglary. I think he was sent to keep an eye on us and prevent the gardener saying too much."

"By who?"

"The taxi driver who directed us to the house, but felt unable to drive us there, preferring that we should take our time. Doesn't that strike you as odd?"

Listening to his friend and watching Jorge Demara becoming visibly agitated, Bingham realised that he would never have provoked the man so speedily, if at all, with so many direct questions and assertions.

"So, you see, Senor Demara …"

"Call me Jorge, please."

"Jorge … we seem to have awoken the wildlife. Now, what do you know? What takes up most of the Spanish police force's time in this neck of the woods?"

"There are criminals here, of course, but they have families and live lives like the rest of us, but the Mayhews had no connection with such people. The police checked that carefully. The English ex-pats live a quiet life. Sun, sea, sand …

"Yes, yes - but?"

"That's what they come here for …"

Jorge ended lamely after Brockie's interruption, his attempt at what he considered joviality stemmed. He paused and looked around the bar, keen, thought Bingham, not to be overheard.

"The kind of people you're talking about own legitimate businesses: clubs, bars, casinos, restaurants, golf courses – that sort of thing," Jorge persisted.

At the mention of golf courses, Bingham smiled at his friend. The ex-policeman ignored him, keeping a straight face, his eyes never leaving the Spanish journalist.

"And they are involved in the housing market. Come on, Jorge, you're a journalist – one of the nosey brigades. What else are they involved in?"

"In the 1990s, house prices doubled. It's was a lucrative business – building and buying property. Some set up as estate agents; many of them invest in timeshares, for example …"

"And where does the money come from?"

"I think you know as well as I do, Mr Brockie."

"So, the building boom here is driven by dirty money?"

"At times."

"I would suggest most of the time. How many of these business deals are carried on under the table?"

"Under the table?"

"Envelopes stuffed with money passed from one person to another while the lawyer overseeing the transaction looks out of the window or tops up the glasses."

"Doesn't that happen everywhere, Simon?"

"There's no chance that the Mayhews were involved in that?" asked Brockie, ignoring the question and the friendship suggested by Jorge's use of his Christian name.

"No. The police were certain they had no criminal record."

"How far are the locals caught up in the drugs trade?"

At the mention of the word 'drugs', Jorge Demara looked round the bar, leaned forward and poured more wine into their glasses.

"It must be tempting for many, bearing in mind Spain's current recession and high unemployment."

"You're a persistent man, Simon."

"And I'll carry on being so until I get some straight answers, Jorge. Let me put a few suggestions to you, bearing in mind that I am now retired and have no official status here or anywhere else. Firstly, you are being cagey about the activities of criminals along this coastline. Secondly, you suspect – if not actually know – more about what might have happened to the Mayhews than you are letting on. Thirdly, you are curious – if not actually knowledgeable – about the identity of the man 'Fred Jackson'. Fourthly ..."

"I take your point, Simon."

"Fourthly, you are definitely perturbed by our presence here and how far we might seem to have progressed in our investigation, or at least how far we might have disturbed the wasps' nest."

Jorge laughed at Brockie's expression, and Bingham was relieved to hear the sound because the tension across the table had mounted, unbearably. Had he faced his friend across an interview desk at a police station back home, Bingham felt that he would have spilled the beans.

"Talking about such things unnecessarily is something we do not do because you never know who's listening and, more to the point, what interpretation they might place on your conversation," said Jorge, "It's not a matter of being 'cagey' but being careful. People have been shot along this coast simply because they *might* have spoken out of turn. The British may refer to us as the Costa del Crime, almost with a laugh at the idea, but here it's been known, since the 1990s when the internal borders came down across Europe, as La Costa del Plomo'.

"The Coast of the Lead Bullet?" said Bingham, speaking for the first time.

"Precisely, Mr Bingham. The Costa has been infiltrated by Serbs, Croats, Russians and Albanians, and the atmosphere here has become increasingly violent. Not long ago a prominent lawyer from Marbella was shot dead for no other reason than that he was exercising his professional duties. He came from a well-respected family in the town. His killing – in front of his wife and child – sent shockwaves through our community. So, you see, we speak with caution, and I would advise you to proceed in the same manner.

You now see why I am 'perturbed' by your presence. This isn't Britain and I feel responsible for your safety. As regards your other 'suggestions', I can only say that I know no more than you about the disappearance of the Mayhews or the identity of Senor Jackson, except that he has lived here many years and is happily married to one of our local women."

"So, you do know him?" said Bingham.

"Yes, very vaguely. I recollect from your description seeing him around the quay."

The journalist's protective tone had changed to one of anger at Bingham's remark, and he stood quickly.

"If I can be of further help, please call my office. Good day, Mr Bingham, Mr Brockie."

Bingham rose and extended his hand, which the Spaniard took. He nodded to Brockie, who remained seated and left the hotel foyer.

"I'm afraid you've upset your daughter's boyfriend, George."

"Yes. I think his anger over his embarrassment was unnecessary. It wasn't my intention to suggest he was lying about not knowing Fred Jackson. After all, as a journalist he must know many people and couldn't be expected to remember them all on the spur of the moment."

"You'd never have made a detective, George. You're too considerate to go for the jugular," said Brockie, with a laugh. "Did you bring your laptop with you, by the way?"

"I always do."

"I'd like to borrow it. I want to make a few enquiries about our Mr Jackson."

Alone in his room and with his notebook in Brockie's hands, Bingham unpacked in his usual ritualistic fashion: trousers colour coordinated with shirts on hangers, pants in one drawer, socks in another, his panama on a shelf, notepad with maps and fountain pen on the desk together with his maps, shoes on the floor of the wardrobe, jackets hung near his shirts but at the other end of the rail.

With a sigh, he removed his clothes and climbed in between the duvet and sheets. It had been a long day and yet it was barely evening. With a quick glance at his watch, noting that this must only be a cat nap, he dropped quickly off to sleep.

He was woken somewhat over two hours later by a repeated banging on his door. He opened it to reveal Simon Brockie, flushed with excitement and bursting with information.

"Had a good kip, George? Us real coppers keep busy while the world sleeps."

"You know who Fred Jackson is?"

"The internet may have revolutionised villainy, but it's also been a big boon to us law enforcement types. I've been in touch with some old friends back home. I tell you, George, if we'd have had Facebook when I started out as a young village copper my patch would have been snow white and squeaky clean. There's nothing you can't find out if you know where to look.

I've also been down to the local police station – if that's the name for the place over here – and had a chat with Lieutenant Palos. Between us, we have our Mr Jackson nicely sewn up."

Bingham made them both a cup of coffee, since he never drank tea abroad, while Brockie expanded on his findings. Patience was one of Bingham's supreme virtues – even Lina acknowledged that to be true – and he waited for the ex-policeman to get to the point.

"Fred Jackson, or Patrick Sims as he was in his Birmingham days, was a drug dealer. Usual story: disruptive family – Patrick on the streets from an early age – bad company – easy money – no thought for the harm he was doing – and so on. Eventually, the inevitable happened and Patrick and his friends get into trouble with a rival gang. There are several skirmishes that end in a number of stabbings and Patrick ends up in gaol.

He doesn't learn his lesson, of course (they never do in the clink) and once out he's dealing drugs again. Only this time, he's peddling the stuff on his own and (wait for it) our Patrick falls in love with one of his customers."

Brockie paused, as though contemplating the manner of his delivery; Bingham thought, as though regretting it.

"The girl died of a heroin overdose supplied by Sims. He found her body in their grubby little flat – arm like a pincushion, needles on the floor. He was devastated and came out here to escape the heartache.

It would have been easy for him to get in with the wrong crowd because the gangs are always looking for mugs to peddle their stuff, but he didn't. The memory of the girl he loved, prostrate on the floor of their flat, brought about a remarkable change in Patrick Sims, who now called himself Fred Jackson. "It's strange, isn't it, how even the most tragic turn of events can have happy endings?

He was lucky, of course. He'd never touched the stuff himself – except for the odd puff – and he met a local woman, a widow with a market stall and a cafe. She gave him a job and eventually married him. She now works him to death – as Lieutenant Palos expressed it – between 'la cama de matrimonio' and 'el mercado'. Even I understood his meaning, George."

Bingham smiled, partly at the Spaniard's humour, partly at the thought of his friend at the police station.

"I take it that Lieutenant Palos spoke good English?"

"Remarkable. These foreigners show us up don't they, George?"

"All the time as far as languages are concerned. Have you erased Mr Jackson from your list of suspects?"

"Not entirely. Let's just say that I view him in a more favourable light."

"I'd have liked to meet this Lieutenant Palos, Brockie."

"Why?"

"I'm not sure. It's just that I'd like to get the feel of the place."

Brockie looked at Bingham as though his friend doubted his competence, but this wasn't Bingham's reason for wanting to meet the lieutenant. It was simply that his instinct told him he must immerse himself in the locality and Lieutenant Palos was part of the picture.

"I'll give him a ring," said Brockie, "I'm sure he'll be only too pleased to meet us for a drink."

"Invite him for an aperativo – somewhere along the quayside."

Lieutenant Palos arrived on the dot and dressed for the evening in a cream suit of American cloth. He was a thin man, on the short side for a policeman thought Bingham, and elegant, with a dainty moustache confined precisely to his top lip. A red handkerchief fluttered from his breast pocket in the warm breeze from the harbour. As he approached, Bingham noticed the reaction of those people already gathered on the quayside, by the boats and in the cafes; everyone noticed the lieutenant and the looks were ones of appreciation rather than contempt or fear: some smiled, others nodded and only one group lounging by their boat muttered among themselves after he had walked by.

Without asking, Lieutenant Palos ordered a bottle of white wine, which came with a selection of shellfish and fingers of toast.

"Eat when you drink, drink when you eat," said the Lieutenant, quoting an old Spanish saying.

Bingham smiled, thinking what a good idea it would be if young, British drunks took similar advice. They talked for a while of the town, the harbour, the restaurants, the food, the local market, the hills and the richness of the Andalusian countryside.

"Water is the key to our beautiful land: water splashing from fountains, water running from our hills, water swelling our crops at night – asparagus, strawberries, tomatoes, peppers, olives, oranges and lemons – and, of course, the sun is ripening everything by day."

Bingham and Brockie listened politely, helping themselves to the tapas, until the conversation came around to the love of the British for this part of Spain and the disappearance of the Mayhews.

"I understand that Colin Mayhew made regular trips to Malaga, Lieutenant."

"That is so."

"Are you able to tell us what they involved?"

"You are very direct, Mr Bingham. Normally our investigations are treated with discretion but, if only because of Senor Brockie's profession, I will confide that the Mayhews owned some property in the city – an apartment or two, I believe – and Senor Mayhew collected the rents."

"Doesn't that strike you as odd in this day and age?"

"They were a couple in their seventies, and not all people of that age are familiar with modern ways. My own parents own a small holiday home in Estepona, and every month they take a trip to collect their rents. It is the way of the old. Besides, Malaga is a pleasant city and

Senor Mayhew no doubt enjoyed the trip. It is less than an hour from here."

"He went alone, though."

"Yes, I believe that was usual. You consider that important?"

"They were a devoted couple, according to their children, always 'locked in each other's arms'. I wondered why Patty Mayhew didn't accompany her husband – if only for a look around the shops."

The lieutenant smiled, obviously understanding Bingham's remark and, therefore, likely to be a married man. Brockie had looked puzzled at Bingham's line of questioning, and now spoke up.

"You wouldn't find a closer couple than you and Lina, George, but you don't go everywhere together; she has her interests and you have yours. I see nothing strange in Colin Mayhew collecting their rents alone."

Bingham said nothing but noted the smile that passed between the two policemen.

"Did you check his movements in Malaga, Lieutenant?"

Lieutenant Palos's smile broadened; Bingham could almost have sworn he winked at Brockie.

"We did, Mr Bingham. He would park in a side street close to both apartments – they were near each other. He would then collect his rents and walk to the Deutsche Bank on the Avenida Andalucia 5 where the rents were deposited in his business account. Afterwards, he made his way to the Café Central on the Plaza de la Constitucion, where he always dined when in Malaga. He ate a leisurely lunch in the Spanish manner, and this was usually a meat dish. Senor Mayhew had a preference for birds: braised quail, marinated pigeon were particular favourites of his when in season."

Bingham returned the lieutenant's broad smile, indicating that he didn't mind being teased; and thinking to himself, in response to Brockie's comment, that Lina wouldn't turn down the chance of a trip to Norwich – also about an hour's drive from home – if he happened to be going that way for any reason.

He detected no undue concern in the lieutenant's light manner; after all, Bingham realised that six hundred people a day go missing in his own country, and the police force couldn't be expected to pursue them all.

Was the heat going from their investigation? Was Fred Jackson just a negligent neighbour? Was Jorge Demara just a provincial journalist who knew nothing more than he'd divulged to Bingham's daughter in what was probably mere gossip?

It was then that chance took a hand. The dry, white wine had gone down well with the seafood and their meeting had come to a natural end when the lieutenant looked up as the shadow of a stranger crossed their table. He stood, quite composed but attentive.

"Senor Garcas," he said, "let me introduce my … colleagues from England: Senor Brockie of the British police and his friend, Senor Bingham."

Senor Garcas smiled so broadly that his face, plump with sun and olives, almost split in two. He hoped that the visitors were enjoying the weather, the food, the countryside and would they excuse Lieutenant Palos for just a moment while he had a word on municipal matters.

The conversation, carried out at a deserted point on the quayside, was brief. Senor Garcas did all the talking and Lieutenant Palos listened, nodding occasionally but not smiling. It was only when he returned to their table that Bingham saw the anger in his eyes and a determined smile on his lips.

"Senor Garcas is the town mayor. He informs me that the law forbids you to ask questions of anyone regarding the disappearance of Senor and Senora Mayhew. According to the statutes, he is right," said Lieutenant Palos, pausing after the word 'statutes', "I bid you good evening, gentleman, and hope you enjoy the rest of the night. I can recommend the Toro Puerto Marina and can anticipate we may meet again."

He left with a friendly wave and a smile. Bingham and Brockie exchanged a glance, acknowledging they had found an ally.

"It's a shame you're a vegetarian, George," said Brockie with a smile.

As it turned out, the Toro Puerto Marina had more to offer than its name suggested.

Chapter Three
RATS OF THE WATERFRONT

Having eaten quite heartily already, Bingham had no desire to reach the restaurant too soon and suggested he and Brockie should enjoy a stroll along the waterfront and the marina. Besides, he wanted a closer look at the bunch of men lounging by their boat who had muttered among themselves when Lieutenant Palos walked by. During their drink with the lieutenant, Bingham had noticed another man join them, and the man was Fred Jackson.

He was no longer there when Bingham and Brockie arrived, but the interest taken by the men in the two friends suggested that they had been the subject of conversation. Given that Jackson's nose was now supposedly clean, Bingham wondered what the discussion might have been about. He refrained from mentioning what he'd noticed to Brockie, whose habit of jumping straight to the point disconcerted Bingham. In his world, nothing was ever as straightforward as it seemed, whereas to Brockie a villain was a villain.

"Buenas tardes, senores."

Bingham's use of 'tardes' rather than 'noches' at that time of the day alerted the men to the fact that he knew something more of their language than the average tourist, had they not already guessed that from their conversation with Fred Jackson.

Bingham proceeded to admire their boat: commenting on its hull, the stacking of the nets, asking about its engine, admiring the cleanness of its lines, enquiring after their catches, inveigling a welcome aboard.

There were six of them in all, surly looking characters, smoking heavily, occasionally spitting into the water. One or two were chewing either gum or tobacco, and all surveyed the two Englishmen with a look of distrust. They were well dressed in matelot-type shirts and designer jeans; three wore jackets in blue serge and one – whose name Bingham elicited as Eusebio Abad – wore a peaked cap of the sort he'd seen on day boat sailors.

But there was nothing of the dilettante about these men: they were all fishermen, hardened by toil, bruised by the Mediterranean Sea where they sought their livelihood. Bingham found himself both admiring and disliking them. There wasn't one he would not have trusted with his life in a storm; there wasn't one he would have wanted to meet in a dark alley at any time of the day.

The boat on which they lounged was clearly the property of Eusebio Abad, to whom the others deferred when talking to Bingham. If one of the others did speak it was with the acknowledgement that Abad was 'el Jefe', which Bingham took to mean 'the Chief'. He was a big man, broad of chest and heavy of muscle. He seemed curious about Bingham and suspicious of Brockie. In his eyes there was both ferocity and gentleness. Bingham could imagine him reading stories to his grandchildren while they sat on his lap and, later in the day, sorting out two sailors angry with drink.

When they moved on, Bingham had secured the promise of a fishing trip and Brockie had determined to make a few enquiries of Lieutenant Palos.

"Villains, George. They may be fishermen but they're also villains."

It was well after 9 o'clock when they arrived at Toro Puerto Marina. The sun was at last going down and its rays shone golden through the restaurant, cutting across the harbour and lengthening the shadows of the boats so that their shapes touched the pontoon on which the restaurant floated. Several tourists were already eating but most of the locals were arriving, gathering at the small podium where a young girl arranged their seating.

Bingham had no desire to eat, since age had diminished his appetite, but Brockie was "as hungry as a horse" and eager to start on the food. While he pored over the menu, Bingham looked around the room.

It was a modern restaurant; much like the hotel foyer, it sported clean lines in metal, glass and plastic and waiters who were equally attentive. Bingham wondered where the Spain of his youth had vanished. For several years after leaving university with his first-class honours' degree in mathematics, Bingham had wandered around Europe, getting to know its people and the four languages that were its main ones at the time. He much preferred the eating places of the side streets: clean but not clinical, their wooden tables and chairs worn down by the years and the locals who were their most frequent customers.

At a far table, deep in conversation, he noticed the town mayor, Senor Garcas, and the ex-drug dealer, Fred Jackson. Leaving Brockie with the menu and a brief apology, Bingham wandered over to renew an old acquaintance and further a new one.

Both men were startled at his approach and disconcerted by his smile. Both stood up, Fred Jackson following Senor Garcas in this exhibition of good manners. The table bore the remains of their meal, which Bingham judged from the stains on the plates to have been a meat stew of some kind accompanied by mixed salads with olives and capers. An empty bottle of an expensive Rioja was placed by the mayor's right hand and both men were enjoying a French brandy. No expense spared, thought Bingham.

"Please excuse me," he said, "I'm sorry to have disturbed your meal. We were only introduced briefly, Senor Garcas. George Bingham."

He extended his hand and the mayor had no option but to take it.

"Alejo Garcas at your service," he replied, with his plump smile.

"My friend and I have no wish to intrude upon your investigation into the disappearance of Senor and Senora Mayhew," said Bingham, "We are here purely in the interests of their family who are naturally concerned as to their whereabouts."

Bingham had intended to say that he and Brockie were there at the request of the Mayhew's family but couldn't quite bring himself to indulge in an outright lie; he hoped the implication might carry the day. He also hoped the mayor might conclude that he was under the impression the Spanish investigation was continuing.

"With Lieutenant Palos, the investigation is in good hands."

"Of course. Is it usual for the Guardia Civil to be concerned in such an investigation? I would have thought the Nacional de Policia …?"

"It is a local matter. It is possible …," said the mayor, interrupting Bingham with a shrug of his shoulders and hovering on the possibility.

Bingham smiled and turned his attention to Fred Jackson, who seemed even more disconcerted than the mayor.

"We meet again, Mr Jackson. Three times must be some kind of record on one's first day in a foreign country."

"Three times?"

"This morning at Colin and Patty's house, at this moment and I noticed you speaking to Senor Abad and his friends – although, I suppose that doesn't quite qualify as a meeting."

The glance that passed between the mayor and the ex-drug dealer was involuntary: neither man could help himself. Had Bingham been a policeman, both would now be on the defensive: the mayor spluttering, the ex-drug dealer antagonistic. But Bingham smiled as though he was pleased to have made such influential acquaintances on the first day of a holiday; he smiled and pursued his line of appreciative familiarity. He spoke in English, occasionally interpreting in case Alejo Garcas had failed to understand, while knowing he understood perfectly.

"Forgive me. You must finish your meal in peace. Perhaps tomorrow we may meet again?"

He directed his last comment to Fred Jackson, guessing that the mayor wanted nothing less than for his dining companion to be involved no further.

"I understand that you and your wife run a café on the waterfront – a charming place. We may well drop in for coffee."

Bingham turned to go and then, as if remembering a plan he'd discussed previously, turned once again to Fred Jackson.

"My friend found a key for you today. Would it be possible to borrow it tomorrow? The family are concerned that certain items ..."

He shrugged as if his meaning was clear to any decent person, directing this to the mayor. Bingham knew he was getting under their skins, needling them to the point where the mayor would have dismissed him, and Jackson might well have struck him had they not been in such a conspicuously public place.

Both men were struggling to keep their composure: the mayor red in the face, his mouth trembling, Jackson flashing angry looks wherever he thought they might have the greatest effect. But Bingham was imperturbable; his smile never faltered as he waited for an answer.

Finally, the mayor took refuge in the hiding place of all bureaucrats – the regulations.

"We should need authorisation from family members and then permission from the Guardia that such a ... a procedure was permissible."

To permit the permissible: Bingham's smiled broadened at the thought. In years gone by obtaining such permission would have taken an inordinate length of time, allowing the case to have grown even colder; nowadays, a simple email would secure the necessary 'permiso'.

"I'll arrange to have it for you in the morning, Senor Garcas."

"I shall need to speak with Lieutenant Palos."

"Naturally, but I am sure the Lieutenant will be only too pleased to accompany us. He is as keen to lay this little mystery to rest as we are to bring comfort to the family."

Once again, Bingham turned to go, moved a foot or two from the dining table and then spun round as though reluctant to leave new-found friends.

"Mr Jackson, as a friend of Colin and Patty's, you must know the people they were expecting for dinner on the day they disappeared. Is it possible I could meet with them?"

He turned to the mayor.

"Not, of course, to question them, to interfere with the investigation, but more to take some small ... degree of solace back to their family at home."

How could the mayor refuse to cooperate; how could any decent person? Bingham watched Fred Jackson look to the mayor. He watched Senor Garcas look away, not wishing to be seen to be consulted. When he received no support, no consent, Fred Jackson took refuge in ignorance.

"I'm not sure if I know who they were expecting that night."

"But you know some of their friends?"

There was a slight nod: a bare agreement that this must be so.

"Did you like the Mayhews?"

Not for the first time in an investigation, Bingham asked a question that came from nowhere and which he was unable, at the time, to explain to himself. Both men at the table looked up at the brusqueness of the query, so out of tune with Bingham's smile and his previous conciliatory manner.

"Of course. There was nothing to dislike. Everyone liked the Mayhews: the other English, the local people," answered Fred Jackson.

"Really, Senor Bingham …"

Bingham didn't allow the mayor to finish. Once on his high horse there would be no stopping the man.

"Then you will have no objection in helping me bring some peace of mind to their family."

It wasn't a question either in intent or tone: it was a trap snapping shut. There were nods and agreements that Bingham hoped would hold good for the next morning. He smiled broadly, obliged each man to shake his hand and returned to Brockie, who sat patiently waiting to order.

"I didn't like to disturb you," he said.

It was only when Brockie was clearing the plate of his dessert and Bingham, who'd declined a sweet course, was regretting having taken the waiter's advice that sherry was "the natural choice for fish" that the ex-policeman said:

"Did you turn up anything else?"

"I don't know. I haven't made up my mind. But I think we might meet with a few of the Mayhew's friends tomorrow – hopefully, those who came to dinner that evening – and we have the chance for another look over their house. I'll need my notebook back, Simon."

Back in his room at La Fonda, Bingham rang his daughter, Fiorenza.

"It won't take you long," he said, in what he hoped was his most persuasive tone. "Anyway, at 28 you're too old for clubbing."

Fiorenza had been about to leave her London flat to go out for the evening with a few girlfriends when Bingham phoned. He'd never understood why anyone would want to go out that late at night and was less than sympathetic when she complained.

He explained that he needed her to contact the Mayhews' family and arrange for them to email him permission to have a look in the villa.

"But Dad they haven't asked you to investigate their parents' disappearance."

"I know, but you can persuade them that it's in everyone's interests that we do. You know more about the details than us. It was on some news channel or other and your journalist boyfriend – who we've met by the way – will have spoken with the family. Wasn't it him who said how close the couple were? Wasn't 'odd' the word used because they were 'always locked in each other's arms'?"

"What did you make of Jorge?"

"I'm not sure."

"What do you mean?"

"I'll tell you when I've made up my mind."

"You've not offended him, have you?"

"Of course not. Jorge was most helpful."

Bingham didn't want to say 'cagey' because the young man had seemed, if anything, frightened. There was a moment's silence on the other end of the line, while Fiorenza decided whether to question her father further. Experience must have told her it was pointless because she said, quite simply:

"You'll have what you need by the morning, Dad. Goodnight for now."

And with that assurance, Fiorenza rang off.

She was as good as her word, and next morning Bingham asked the receptionist at the hotel to print off the necessary email for him. As soon as he and Brockie had finished breakfast they set off to find Lieutenant Palos and Fred Jackson.

The lieutenant was formal in his manner but clearly pleased that the mayor had been outmanoeuvred. He eyed the email cursorily, nodded and led the way to the café owned by Fred Jackson's wife.

It was a neat place: small and tidy with red gingham tablecloths and the over-riding smell of early morning coffee and hot chocolate that was being served with churros – the long strips of fried batter, which local customers were dipping in their drinks. On the counter, shielded from the flies by mesh covers, Bingham noticed an assortment of rolls: ensaimados and sobaos among them.

Senora Jackson, who Fred introduced as Imelda, was hot and busy but pleased to see "the English gentlemen". Whether or not this welcome excluded Lieutenant Palos, Bingham wasn't sure, but the policeman seemed unperturbed.

Fred Jackson, clearly disgruntled but in awe of his wife, jotted the names and addresses required onto a waiter's notepad, tore off the sheet and handed it to Bingham, who showed the names to the lieutenant who, in turn, nodded approval.

"We have spoken with these people," he said, with a shrug, "but who knows! Would you prefer to walk, gentlemen, or shall I arrange for us to be driven to the villa? I am assuming you want to look over the Mayhews' home first."

"I'm happy to walk," replied Bingham.

"Or we might try the taxi of the driver who felt unable to take us yesterday," suggested Brockie, smiling at the lieutenant who returned the acknowledgement that professionals never missed a trick.

"Yes, I hadn't thought of that idea," said Bingham.

As they left the quayside and made their way uphill into the town, Bingham turned to look at the sun as it rose above the outlying houses of Guaro del Mar, shafting its golden light across the harbour, throwing the dark shadows of morning over the still water. The windows of the houses and the boats glistened, and their bright colours shone. His friends had moved on, not noticing Bingham's distraction, and so it was only he who saw the young man approach the boat of Eusebio Abad, only he who saw a package pass between the two. He noticed the camaraderie of the men – the slap on the young man's shoulder and the appreciative toss of his head – and Bingham made a sudden decision.

Catching the others up, he asked if they would view the villa without him and, perhaps, speak to the Mayhews' friends. When asked why, he muttered something about Abad's boat and left in a hurry in case he should miss the young man's departure. When he arrived back on the corner of the street, Abad had disappeared into his boat and the young man was making his way along the waterfront and into the town.

Bingham followed at a leisurely pace, gathering his thoughts as he went. Having decided on this course of action, he wasn't sure where it might lead. He might get into conversation with the young man; on the other hand, there was no reason to suppose the young man would have any desire to get into conversation with him.

The youth walked in a determined manner: whatever his business had been with Abad, it didn't appear to be the end of his morning's work. There was purposefulness in his step, and Bingham soon found himself hurrying along in a way no tourist would have done.

The streets narrowed, small plazas appeared with fountains at the centre and surrounded by shops. Occasionally the young man would enter one but did not stay for long and Bingham had no occasion to see whether he handed over any more packages.

The open plazas and the busy streets became alleyways, dark passages, footpaths and scores as the youth twisted and turned through the town, appearing to be making his way back to the harbour. It was in one of these smaller thoroughfares that Bingham bumped into him. The youth was standing in the shadow of an arch and blocked Bingham's path.

"Hello," he said, "Are you following me by any chance?"

Chapter Four
TOUCH OF BRAVADO

"Yes," replied Bingham, "I was trying to … "

"Catch me up?"

"Yes, catch you up … somewhere …

"Somewhere? Where?"

"Where we might have a quiet word. I think you might be able to help me."

"You could have just called out. I'm not deaf."

"No, I … didn't like to do that – not us being strangers and this being …"

"A strange place? You can say that again, mate. I don't like being followed. It makes me feel uneasy. I'll tell you what. Two plazas back there's a little café. How about us meeting there in, say, half an hour?"

Bingham could see that he had no choice; this time, he was the one who had been outmanoeuvred. The youth might simply vanish, but there was nothing Bingham could do, not against someone who held all the cards, not against someone who was filling in his pauses for him.

"Thank you," he said, "I'll be waiting."

"You do just that – and remember I don't like being followed. You get me?"

Sitting in the little café two plazas back, Bingham suddenly realized that their conversation had been conducted in English. He also realised that he had known all along that the youth was a Brit, and yet he looked local.

The café seemed to be the extension of a kitchen that simply opened onto the plaza. As soon as he sat down, a fat woman approached, her face smiling, and offered him coffee. It came with the seemingly inevitable toast and a small pot of honey. Had he been holidaying, Bingham would have enjoyed the moment even more than he did.

It was almost on the half hour that the youth arrived and sat opposite Bingham. The woman placed a cola before him, which he downed in one gulp. Not a word passed between them. Bingham watched the youth, wishing his own hair was still jet black and curling round his ears.

"Now, what can I do for you?"

"My name's George Bingham, and you are?"

"Richard Brown. That surprised you, didn't it?"

"I'd somehow guessed you were British, although I can't think why. You look every inch the Spaniard."

"I've lived here all my life. I was born here. That's been part of the problem."

"Your parents live here?"

"No. That's part of the problem."

"You seem young to be going it entirely alone."

"It's sink or swim here, mate, I can tell you."

"Do you have no friends or relations here at all?"

"No – not even a girlfriend."

"I'm sorry to hear that. In all my seventy-two years, I've never really been alone. I wandered round Europe when I was about your age but, even then, I seemed to make friends wherever I stopped off for a while."

"How old do you think I am?"

"Twenty ... five?"

Richard Brown looked at Bingham, the expression on his face a mixture of awe and mistrust. His whole demeanour, but especially the tone of his voice, had been offhand. It hadn't occurred to him, although it had to Bingham, that he had been the topic of conversation rather than Bingham's reason for following him.

"How'd you know?"

"During my working life I was a teacher. You get used to guessing young people's ages, I suppose. So, where are your parents?"

"Back home."

The touch of bravado was back. Here was a boy, thought Bingham, left by his parents in Spain for whatever reason, who had gone it alone, and was proud of the fact.

"But you're not here to find out about me, are you?"

It was both a challenge and a question; the youth, in some respects, hoped that was exactly why Bingham was in Guaro del Mar, whereas, in his heart of hearts, he knew it wasn't.

Bingham wondered whether to pursue his line of enquiry or to get to the point; but it was Richard Brown who decided.

"I saw you following me early on. I thought for a bit that you were a copper, but I knew even a British copper would know how to follow someone without being seen. So, who are you and what do you want?"

"You have reason to dislike British policeman?"

"Never mind that! I've done nothing wrong over there. I've never been over there. But, yes, I've come across them here."

"Why?"

"I said never mind. What do you want of me?"

"I was on the quayside this morning when I saw you handing a package to a man called Eusebio Abad ..."

"El Jefe?"

"Yes. Last night, he was in conversation with another man who knows, or did know, two people who have gone missing ..."

"The Mayhews?"

"Yes."

"You're looking for them?"

"Yes."

"Are you a private detective or something?"

"No. I heard about Colin and Patty Mayhew's disappearance from my daughter, who works for the BBC, and it seemed sad that two people of their age should simply go missing. I thought I'd take a look."

"Oh, you did, did you? You might have bitten off more than you can chew, mate."

"You're the second person who's said that to me."

"And who was the other one?"

"A friend of mine. He's with me. In fact, he's looking over the Mayhews' house at this very moment."

"How long have you been here?"

"Since yesterday morning."

"What do you want with me?"

"I'm not sure I want anything. You obviously know Senor Abad and he knows ... this other gentleman who we met yesterday. I thought there might be a chance you knew the Mayhews as well and could help us find them."

"No."

"No what?"

"No, I can't."

"But you do know them – or, at least, you've heard of them?"

"Everyone's heard of them."

"Disappearances round here aren't an everyday occurrence?"

"You don't half speak posh, don't you? But there you'd be wrong – disappearances round here *are* an everyday occurrence! And that's why you don't ask questions."

"Whether you answer or not is up to you, Richard. My friend and I have no official business here, but we intend to keep asking questions until we get some answers."

Bingham wasn't sure whether it was his use of the young man's Christian name or his quiet persistence but, whatever the reason, Richard Brown suddenly seemed mollified.

"You're nothing to do with the police?"

For one very brief second, Bingham wondered whether he should acknowledge Brockie's previous occupation; he decided against the idea, since he and Richard Brown seemed to be getting somewhere.

"No. My friend and I are here just to find Colin and Patty Mayhew. When that's done, we shall be off home."

Bingham glanced at the proprietress who brought another cola and another coffee. She also placed a plate of rosquillos on the table, and Bingham dunked one while he waited.

"I've had to make my own way over here. Mum and Dad came over just after I was born. They were fed up with England and had a bit of money put by. Housing was cheaper then and they just kept re-mortgaging when they needed a bit extra. Property prices were going up and up, and it wasn't a problem. It wasn't a problem until about nine or ten years ago when the recession hit us. House prices dropped. Mum and dad owed more than they could pay, and they scarpered back to the UK. They live with relatives now."

"Why didn't you go? You must have been about fifteen at the time."

"Sixteen. What was over there for me? I'd never really lived in the UK. I didn't know anyone. I went to school here. All my friends were here and most of them stayed behind."

Once again, Bingham realised what a protected life he'd led and how he and Lina had cossetted their own children, free as they had been to make their own choices and live their own lives. He recalled teasing Fiorenza about her clubbing at twenty-eight.

"What did you do? How did you earn your keep?"

"It was a nightmare. I won't deny that. Even jobs as waiters are hard to come by because the restaurants and cafes are family run … I suppose you might say I struck it lucky. I'd smoked a bit of hash when I was at school, like most kids, but I hadn't got hung up on it. I saw what it did to you – slowing you down and making you apathetic. But a lot of my friends did and through them I met their hash dealer, Pete. Yeah, he was a Brit, too.

Anyway, he needed a runner and said he'd pay me a weekly salary if I worked for him. I jumped at the chance. I'd been living on the streets until then, finding my dinner from the bins behind the restaurants. With a regular income, I could look the world in the face again. I got a flat with some mates and my future looked rosy. I don't suppose you'd see it that way, would you Mr Bingham? But it's a lot better than some of the things my friends have had to do. Two of the girls I was at school with work in brothels. They don't like it, but it's the only way they can make a living."

Bingham felt glad that he'd met Richard Brown. There was no doubt he was a 'hard case' (as the expression has it) but he was also little more than a boy in many ways and was only too pleased to be talking to someone about his life. During his years as a teacher and particularly ever since his first investigation, Bingham had realised how people needed to talk.

"Go on," he said.

"One day, Pete just disappeared. I don't know why. I didn't stay to find out. Some Albanians moved in on his patch and I was gone. You don't stay around to wonder why with those bastards, I can tell you. I was on the streets again. I slept in doorways, on the beaches – anywhere I could lay my head. Even my old friends didn't want to know me. They'd look the other way when I passed them in the street.

I knew I had to get things together, and the only way I knew was selling hash. I knew Pete's suppliers and thought if I was careful to steer clear of what had been his patch, I might build up a clientele of my own. Everyone smokes hash around here. It's no different from having a cigarette or a drink of alcohol.

That was it, really. It didn't take me long – about a couple of years and I was on my feet again. Most of my customers are ordinary people like me and you. They don't want trouble and neither do I. I make sure I steer clear of anyone likely to cause me hassle. I'm careful not to poach on other people's territory. I'm putting money by in the bank. When I've got enough, I'm giving up the hash business before it gives me up."

"And is it likely to give you up?"

"The dealers who are clever never stay in the game too long. I reckon that was Pete's problem. I don't know; I'm just guessing. But I do know that another bloke who was a small dealer like me didn't know when to stop and he got a very clear message ..."

Richard paused as though not sure whether to relate the incident, perhaps wondering whether he'd already said too much; but Bingham was quiet, almost laid back, and his silence encouraged confidences from those who wanted to talk.

"He'd built up a large clientele, some of them from the richer parts of town, and these Serbs must have got to hear of it. They moved in on his patch and told him that from now on he'd be working for them. Well, he didn't take the hint and told them to fuck off. He hadn't worked hard to hand over his livelihood to a group of gangsters. You can't blame him, can you? These foreigners have got a bloody cheek. Anyway, a couple of days later they paid him a visit. No by your leave: they just kicked open his door and shot him. He wasn't killed. The bullet passed right through his mouth and out the other side. He was lucky, but he hasn't felt up to working since."

The touch of bravado was back in Richard Brown's vocabulary and manner of delivery: a hard man in a tough world and he wanted Bingham to know it.

Bingham thought the young man had finished his story and there were still questions he wanted to ask. How well did he know the Mayhews, if at all? Were they clients of his? Was his relationship with Senor Abad more than was obvious? Did he know Fred Jackson? But the young man hadn't finished. His story, as well as a kind of confession, had also been delivered as a warning: a warning the younger man clearly enjoyed dishing out to the older.

"One of my suppliers is a copper," he said, "a local bloke. He approached me through a customer. The police confiscate loads of hash, as you might guess, and it's supposed to be burnt, but that doesn't always happen – at least not to all of it. This copper said that it was easy to get hold of even large lumps of the stuff. I thought at first that he was setting me up, although I'm too small to bother with when you consider what the police are up against, but no – he was genuine and he's now one of my regular suppliers. You want to tread carefully, Mr Bingham."

"You think that the Mayhews were involved with drugs?"

"I didn't say that because I don't know. They certainly weren't customers of mine and no one has ever suggested that they were involved in any way, but they have disappeared, and no one seems eager to find them, do they? Is there anything else you want to know? I'm a busy man."

"Do you know a man who calls himself Fred Jackson?"

"What do you mean – 'calls himself'? He is Fred Jackson."

"So, you know him?"

"Yes," replied Richard Brown, after a brief hesitation, and then added, "Everyone knows Fred."

"Why?"

"He's married to one of the local women."

"I imagine many other Brits are, too, but why does everyone know Fred in particular?"

"Fred's clean. I know that for a fact."

"I wasn't suggesting he wasn't. I'm just curious as to why everyone seems to know him – the Mayhews, a journalist I've met, Eusebio Abad, a young gardener, a member of the Guardia and even the town mayor."

"When did you say you got here – yesterday morning? You've been about a bit, Mr Bingham."

"I keep bumping into people."

"Well you make sure you don't bump into the wrong ones."

It was more of a warning than a threat but held no meaning for Bingham either way. He was quite taken with the young man, whose tanned and ruddy cheeks and mop of dark, curly hair spoke to him of youth and the future. He'd always felt protective of young people – perhaps an off-shoot of his profession, perhaps the reason for his choice of it – and there was something about this boy (Bingham couldn't think of him as a man), his freshness and his vitality, that appealed to Bingham's age.

They sat quietly for a while, neither uncomfortable with the silence as though they'd known each other for years. Eventually Bingham said:

"Thank you for speaking with me. I don't know that I've learned anything definite, but I now have a picture of the town in my head. It may help."

He reached into his jacket pocket and removed a leather-bound notebook he always carried. On it he wrote his telephone number, tore out the page and handed it to Richard Brown.

"If ever you do make it to the UK and need help, give me a ring and I'll see what I can do."

Richard Brown stared at Bingham before taking the piece of paper and seemed uncertain as to whether this was trap or whether the old man was just a fool. He seemed on the verge of tears as he rose, offered his hand and said goodbye.

Bingham watched him stride off across the plaza and disappear beneath one of the many arches that surrounded the place. He felt disinclined to move: the coffee and the sun had got to him and Bingham wondered whether he might sit where he was all day, enjoying salt-basted sea bass for lunch and dozing through the afternoon.

It was as his eyes closed that he saw the figure moving towards him. He'd noticed it about half an hour before – the faded jeans, the yellow-striped shirt and the peaked sailor's cap – but the person had been too far away for Bingham's old eyes to recognise who it was; Fred Jackson was within a few feet of him before Bingham realised it was the reformed drug dealer.

"Mr Bingham, we meet again."

"And not by accident I think."

"Sorry?"

"You've been loitering on the other side of the plaza for at least thirty minutes if I'm not mistaken. Did you follow me here?"

"You have sharp eyes for a man of your age, Mr Bingham."

"I'm afraid not. I didn't recognise you. It was just your clothes I saw as a blur of colour."

Fred Jackson laughed, acknowledging a shared sense of humour.

"I saw you leave the quayside following young Brown."

"After he'd dropped off el Jefe's hash?"

"Yes. Mr Bingham, I'll be frank with you. You're a dangerous man – not because of what you think you know but because of your ignorance. I know young Brown and I know what he's been through. Talking with you – a man who is nosing around where nosing around is not advisable – could place him in the gravest danger.

You know nothing of the darker side of the Costa, and I'd advise you now to look no further. Enjoy a round or two of golf with your policeman friend and then go home to your wife and children. That's what tourists do in Guaro del Mar. Be a tourist for all our sakes."

With that string of advice, Fred Jackson was off across the plaza following in the footsteps of young Brown. Yet again, the words came to Bingham more as a warning than a threat: in fact, decidedly an appeal.

He paid for the drinks, thanked the proprietress for the wine pastries and walked slowly back towards the quay.

Brockie and Lieutenant Palos must have looked over the Mayhews' villa by now; it was time to find out what they'd discovered – if anything. They'd arranged no meeting place, and so Bingham made for the quayside where he found el Jefe and his friends lounging by their boat. They were dressed much as they had been the previous day. In fact, the whole scene before Bingham was like a still life – 'still' being the operative word. Nothing seemed to have changed since yesterday: the boats, the cafes, the houses, the small beacons flashing on the harbour wall, the undisturbed surface of the sea and the lazing of the people. It was mid-morning; the heat was building, and the world was motionless.

Bingham stood for a while in the shadow of a netting shed. No one had noticed his arrival. He waited, watching the group of fishermen, hoping they would make a move. Words passed between them, there was laughter of the kind shared at a ribald joke and eventually the men sauntered over to one of the bars that lined the quayside.

Bingham watched them settle to their beers and then he joined them. The men glanced at him as his beer was brought across by the young waitress, acknowledging his presence by a closing of their eyes rather than a gesture of the hand or the voice. Only Eusebio Abad touched his cap in what might have been a welcome but could easily have been to relax the cap on his forehead.

Two of the men brought out packets of cigarettes and began to smoke luxuriously, drawing the smoke deep into their lungs before exhaling slowly through pursed lips. Abad lit a cigar, while the others settled for pipes. Occasionally, a remark was passed but no conversation followed. Bingham was aware that the remarks were directed at him, but his deafness made it impossible to hear what was said. Laughter would follow the remarks.

The young waitress frowned at the men and brought Bingham a plate of pastries. He accepted her courtesy with a smile and stretched his legs full length beside the table in a relaxed manner. He spoke a word or two with her, commenting on how pretty he thought her hair looked shining in the sun. It was as black as coal, much like Fiorenza's and Lina's when she was younger. Bingham said so to the young woman who blushed, smiled and asked him about his family. They spoke until other customers arrived and she attended to her duties.

The fishermen had listened to the conversation, straining to hear because Bingham had deliberately dropped his voice and the young woman's was soft by nature. They now nudged each other, possibly speculating – thought Bingham – on what an old Englishman might have wanted from a young, Spanish waitress.

These men were part of the underbelly of the town; Bingham was sure of his suspicions. Their whole manner was one he considered to be subdued arrogance: the kind of knowingness that might or might not be a threat. He admitted to himself, as he sipped his beer and savoured the pastry rings, that el Jefe and his friends frightened him more than the young drug dealer with whom he'd spent most of the morning.

He noticed one of the men approaching the café proprietor. Words were passed between him and the young waitress who shrugged her shoulders, tossed her black hair and dismissed them both with a brief comment and a scornful laugh, before coming to Bingham to ask if he wanted another beer.

The fisherman returned to el Jefe's table. There was a grumbled conversation, much frowning and some fierce glances in Bingham's direction. He was pleased they seemed to have been needled, but whether by him or the young woman Bingham was unsure.

Chapter Five
DETERMINED TO TALK

Bingham was still sitting outside the café and on his third beer when Brockie arrived back at the quayside. He was alone. It was a disappointment to Bingham that the lieutenant was not with his friend: a little more needling might have gone a long way. But the ex-policeman's arrival did stir the pot considerably. Whether it was because knowledge of his previous profession had leaked out or whether it was simply Brockie's manner and bearing, Bingham was left to ponder as he watched the reactions of the fishermen and beckoned to the young waitress.

"May we see a menu, sweetheart," he said with a smile, "My friend and I are eating early. We've got a busy afternoon ahead of us."

He knew the young woman had taken his side out of pure defiance of her employer and the fishermen and assumed she might pass on this information in the same spirit.

They both ordered a seafood paella and Brockie joined his friend by ordering further beers.

"Well?" asked Bingham.

"Nothing other than you'd expect. There were several savings accounts but no extraordinary amounts of money. The business account was exactly as you'd expect from the rents gathered. They were entered once a month, every month, on the day Colin Mayhew collected them. The current account showed the same regular amounts withdrawn each week. No money was stashed anywhere in the house …"

"You did search everywhere that was likely?"

"George …"

"I'm sorry. Of course, you did. You weren't a copper all those years for nothing."

"And nor was our Lieutenant Palos. He's a good man, George. I believe his investigation went as far as it could and got nowhere. This narks him no end, and he's very pleased that we've arrived to annoy people. How did you get on?"

"Don't rush me, Simon. Where is the lieutenant?"

"He needed to get back to work."

"Why?"

"He wanted to see the mayor's reaction."

"Relief or annoyance?"

"Precisely."

"Did you get a chance to speak with the Mayhews' friends?"

"Yes."

"Was the Lieutenant with you?"

"Why do you ask?"

"Was he?"

"Yes. George, I can assure you that Palos is straight."

"What did their friends have to say?"

"Nothing more than we already knew from your daughter's account. They arrived at a quarter to six, waited for a while, and when Colin and Patty failed to turn up, they phoned the family, knowing Patty's habit of ringing home on a Sunday evening."

"How did they get to the villa?"

"They walked – two couples from that little, hillside development that stretches beyond the Mayhews' villa, and the Spanish couple, Senor and Senora Higuera from the town."

"And they walked?"

"Yes, along the only road from Guaro del Mar that leads to the villa. No vehicles passed them on the way in either direction and no vehicles passed the English couples on their way down."

"Did they arrive together?"

"You're beginning to think like a copper, George – be careful! I wondered myself whether the Higuera's might have been involved in some way. They arrived after the English couples at about six o'clock."

Bingham was silent for a while. The onion and garlic had been fried until golden and the peppers and tomatoes had simmered nicely in the kitchen of the café as they were talking. Bingham could smell the saffron and wine as it was added with the stock to the rice. He hoped the cook had remembered to leave out the chorizo. She would soon be adding the peas, the prawns, the mussels and the clams. Lunch was a quarter of an hour or so away

The young waitress brought them another two beers without being asked, and Bingham – despite the beer being of the weak Spanish type – was beginning to feel lightheaded. Each time they came close to some kind of answer they seemed, at the same moment, to drift away.

He thought back over what young Richard Brown had said and relayed the information to Brockie.

"So, he's going straight, is he, once he's made enough money from villainy?"

Bingham didn't argue with his friend. He supposed that he might have taken the same line had he spent his life as a policeman chasing the likes of Richard Brown. But he hadn't: as a teacher, his attitudes had been forged in a different furnace. He didn't approve of Richard Brown's means of earning a living but was grateful that neither he nor his own children had ever found themselves facing the same predicament.

The paella arrived with more beers and for the remainder of their lunch hour the two friends ate in silence. The paella was spectacular. Bingham doubted whether even Lina could have produced one as good. The bed of rice was scented with the saffron and the wine, the flavours of the shellfish permeated the dish and the vegetables were succulent. But it was more than the skills of the cook: it was the smell of the seafront, the fishermen and their nets, the Spanish sun on their backs. Nobody in the world makes paella like the Spanish.

Bingham was careful to wipe up every trace of juice from his plate with the bread provided and this met with the approval of the waitress and the cook who Bingham went to thank. She was a small woman, rounded and glowing with olive oil, her hair black and glistening as the wing of a young raven.

She was younger than Bingham by many years but spoke to him as though she was his mother, placing her hand on his arm as she drew him aside into the rear of the kitchen, determined to talk with him. He was taken by surprise and aware that the woman was speaking despite her husband, the patron. There was a deep sense of urgency in her voice and her concerns for his safety were whispered in the Spanish of the south with its deep, rustic dialect; several times, Bingham had to assure her that he understood what she was saying.

Once again, he had a sense of foreboding. He heard the voices of decent people desiring only to get on with their lives unhampered by villainy. It was as though their town had been infiltrated and occupied by a foreign, virulent power.

Brockie saw his concern when Bingham returned to the table. They left their payment for the meal with a large tip for the young waitress and nodded to her as they left. Bingham watched her clear the dishes and throw him a smile. As she did so, the fishermen returned to their boats.

"It's time to put the squeeze on someone, Simon."

"On your journalist friend?"

"Yes. You're better at it than I am. Let's seek him out."

Jorge Demara wasn't difficult to find. A phone call took Bingham and Brockie to one of the plusher bars that lined the main street of the town, the street that ran parallel to the seafront, and they found him lounging in one of the easy chairs reading his own newspaper. He rose with a smile that Bingham decided was too ready and shook them both warmly by the hand: again, Bingham decided, too warmly.

"How are your investigations progressing?"

"We've come to the point where we need to ask you the same question," replied Brockie, "It seems unbelievable to me that your own didn't progress further than you have cared to acknowledge so far. Given that we've been in Guaro only twenty-four hours and that the trail is old we seem to have aroused more interest than you did at the time of the Mayhews' disappearance.

Come on, Senor Demara, open up. You know you want to."

The Spaniard looked around him in the same nervous manner he had displayed when they first met: his tan faded, his thick hair became lank and his eyes lost their sparkle. Brockie was merciless.

"We've been followed, watched and warned off by at least half a dozen people. Why? There's no evidence the Mayhews were involved in anything illegal – or is there?"

"I've told you – no!"

"But were they? Come on, man, if you're a real journalist you must have dug something up. Who were they connected with? What are you frightened of? Names!"

Jorge's eyes flitted across and caught Bingham's quiet gaze. His professional competence had been held in question and he had now been called a coward. Bingham saw Fiorenza's smile and the Spaniard's manhood slipping away. Brockie drove home the knife.

"Who is the copper who supplies hash to the pushers?"

"You're on the wrong track."

"Then take a grip on yourself and divert us to the right one."

"Those of us who live here love our country. We are proud of our heritage, of our being poised between Africa and Europe. We are a rich and diverse people. One early explorer described us as 'being poised between the hat and the turban'. We celebrate our culture, our fiestas – and we have three thousand each year. The local saints' days are occasions for dressing up and for parades. Every incident in the history of our towns is a reason for processions, feasting with our neighbours, for parades and for crowds in the street. We greet the seasons with affection ... When the English came, we even greeted them. We made them welcome, we built them homes and we invited them to join us: another invasion, another reason for celebration.

But with the good there always comes the bad. British gangsters made their homes here. I've told you how they invested their money in real estate, in golf courses, in casinos ... and so on. But even they settled down and became part of the local scene: their children attended local schools and they contributed generously to municipal events.

The situation here had settled into a steady pattern until two things occurred: the removal of borders across Europe and the recession. Gangs from Russia, Serbia, Bulgaria and Albania didn't share the same respect for our traditions: with them there was no 'honour among thieves', as you call it. Even your criminal elements have a code of conduct – certain rules by which they live: they did not poach on someone else's territory, they respected women, they did not push their way into the lives of the local people ... and so on."

Bingham sensed that Brockie was becoming more and more irritated with Jorge's ramblings and cast his friend a quick glance. Much as he himself liked to capture the feel of the local scene, Bingham, too, felt that the journalist's brush was more concerned with camouflage than enlightenment.

"I am coming to the point," said Jorge, catching the glance, "Give me a moment. I have already said how the gangs from Eastern Europe have caused trouble, but it is the recession that has made it worse. Everyone is now struggling to make a living. In the past these gangs could make a healthy profit from their businesses and invest their money; today, the profit margins are squeezed so tightly that there is little room for manoeuvre. There's less money, much less money than there was, to spend. People who have done business with each other for years are now fighting for survival and fighting against each other."

"Gang wars?" said Brockie, quietly.

"Yes, and all of us are trying to stay out of their path."

"Senor Demara, are you trying to tell us that even the locals and the British ex-pats are finding themselves drawn into this conflict," said Bingham.

"You have said several times that the Mayhews – and it is only Patty and Colin we're concerned with – were not involved," persisted Brockie.

"I could find no evidence that they were."

"And neither could Lieutenant Palos."

"No … he is a very thorough officer."

The pause was only slight, but it was enough for an experienced policeman.

"But?"

"But nothing, Senor Brockie."

"Are you suggesting that the police investigation was flawed?"

"No! I am suggesting that people do not want to be drawn into this … this whirlpool of intrigue and crime."

"But we are drawn, Senor Demara, whether we like it or not. Colin Mayhew knew Eusebia Abad, didn't he? The fisherman would sometimes take him out on his boat. Was he offering advice as to weather conditions and where best to fish? They were familiar. Am I right? Did they know just a little about each other's business? Fred Jackson – as he calls himself – was also known to the Mayhews. You don't seem surprised at my suggestion that Fred Jackson may be an alias. Did you investigate his past? I imagine so. Any thorough journalist would have done so without thinking twice about it. And tell us precisely why Senor Garcas is keen to restrain our investigation."

Jorge Demara laughed.

"You English have a way of propelling events forward at great speed, but that is not our way. Given time, the dust will settle, all eventualities will fall into place. Your gangsters have been part of our life here for decades and now those from Eastern Europe are claiming the life of our town, but they, too, will settle down. At the moment, they are content to drop their families off in the UK to live on the benefits you provide, but the day will come when they want them here. There is something to be said for allowing the criminal underworld to destroy itself. Please let me complete what I have to say."

His last remark was directed at Brockie, who had raised a restraining hand, eager to intervene.

"It may well be that things will get worse before they get better. Certainly, many of the newcomers have little regard for human life. But most of them are stupid. What they do not seem to understand is that the more violent they become the less likely it is that their businesses will remain viable. Where there is no demand, it matters not who controls the supply."

As the Spanish journalist expounded a different world view, they listened, but impatiently.

"Once you have been here for more than the time it takes for your jet lag to wear off you will notice that the bars and the restaurants and the clubs – once thriving businesses – are closing down or have already done so. No longer are customers spilling out onto the pavements soaking up the evening sunshine. Last season, a restaurant called the Trocadero was full of families – some locals, many tourists and businessmen."

Jorge Demara paused on the last word, as though he was still unsure whether or not Bingham and Brockie were receiving his message.

"The businessmen were your fellow countrymen. What their *business* was we never discovered but they were clearly the target of a gang of Serbs who simply drove past the Trocadero and sprayed it with bullets. It didn't matter to these gangsters that perfectly innocent people were in the restaurant enjoying a meal together; life must be very cheap in their homeland."

Bingham suddenly became aware that he was very tired. He felt that listening to the journalist was like trying to hold a conversation with someone passing by on a carousel as one stood watching it whirl round. Normally a polite man – polite almost to the point of self-parody, Lina had once said – Bingham, nevertheless, rose abruptly and walked away, leaving Brockie and Demara gazing after him.

The town was quiet as he emerged from the bar. Bingham was tempted to make for the harbour but turned instead up a side street. He was soon lost in the old town that clung to the hillside to the east of the new buildings, where the Mayhews and their friends lived. It was a walk of instinct rather than design, driven by a desire to get away from the journalist before Bingham lost his temper.

There was poverty here – Bingham could see that clearly – but there was also pride: rundown, yes, in that most of the dwellings would have benefitted from a fresh lick of paint, but there was no graffiti, no weeds growing through the cracks in the pavements. The people cared about their neighbourhood.

Did the Mayhews ever wander here: did their friends? Was the area policed? How did the locals feel about the Brit invasion? Brockie had turned up nothing from his conversation with the Higueras. No one outside their immediate circle seemed to know the Mayhews, and yet they had lived here for twenty years. Someone must have known them well enough to abduct them if they were abducted. It didn't seem credible that they had simply walked out.

Bingham strolled on and found himself in the very plaza where he had spoken with Richard Brown that morning. He was about to find a seat in the small café where the fat woman had been so generous with her rosquillos and coffee when he saw Lieutenant Palos walking towards him. The policeman held out his hand and Bingham took it.

"Did you find out what you wanted to know from Senor Demara?"

Was it the case that everyone wanted them to understand they couldn't make a move without it being noticed? Bingham decided not to ask the question.

"He told us about the killings in the Trocadero. You must often feel frustrated, Lieutenant Palos. Your job here is not an enviable one."

The policeman's awkwardness was apparent, and he was not made more comfortable by Bingham's kindly and understanding tone. Bingham had read somewhere that the Latin male temperament found failure difficult to accept, that such men could not tolerate seeing themselves as losers. It was an attitude that had been responsible for botching many an investigation: false arrests, manufactured evidence, hurried accusations, wild assumptions and the indiscriminate scattering of blame. But Lieutenant Palos was a man of dignity: a man capable of lifting himself above the common rut.

"Did you really locate no one connected with the Mayhews? I find that difficult to believe, Lieutenant, when speaking with a man of your obvious calibre."

The lieutenant did not answer, not so much as by a twitching of his elegant moustache. The impassivity of his face was due to indecision or embarrassment, but Bingham could not make up his mind one way or the other. He persisted, hoping for a breakthrough.

"There must have been certain suspects both here and in Malaga."

Still the policeman didn't answer. Bingham resisted the temptation to trot out a list of names. He didn't want to offer the policeman a means of retreat into denial; he wanted to challenge the man's sense of competency, but not outright, not in condemnation.

The two men stood in the plaza, the business of the cafes and small shops going on around them, each waiting for the other to give way, Bingham with his questions, the policeman with his pride. Afterwards, Bingham decided it was mutual respect that turned the key, a respect built in trust, a trust based on some concept of honour.

The policeman took a notebook from his pocket, tore free a page and wrote one name upon it: Liam Paisley. Underneath the name he wrote an address. He hesitated for some time before handing the piece of paper to Bingham.

"Be careful," he said, smiled briefly and walked on his way.

Chapter Six
LINK TO THE MISSING COUPLE

It was a rundown area of Guaro del Mar in which Bingham found himself: rundown but modern. It appeared to have been a housing estate built for the invasion of the Brits but was now abandoned. Swimming pools, dry and cracked, were filled with windblown litter; weeds had taken over the pavements and roads; some windows were bordered up but the planks had been yanked aside where a squatter sought refuge from the night or an addict looked for a place to indulge their habit; once sparkling paintwork was now dull and peeling; the neatly planted shrubberies were overgrown with dry, yellow grass and the bushes were in need of pruning; ivy was creeping over walls and roofs.

Bingham thought back to what he'd been told about the recession. These properties had probably been financed by gangsters eager to place their ill-gotten gains in some legitimate business. With a smile, Bingham thought to himself that their investments had come to this array of ruins. He decided there must be thirty or more houses on the estate, but all were now lifeless. Well, not quite all: Liam Paisley lived in one of them.

He knocked at the door whose number he'd been given, having eased aside several beer cans and wrappers from fast food packets that barred his way. The driveway looked as though the dustbin had blown over one night and no one had bothered to tidy up.

He was not surprised by the face or the smell that greeted him when a man, dressed only in a dirty singlet and whose hair looked in need of a good wash, opened the door.

"Mr Paisley?"

The man stared at Bingham, for what he later decided could not have been less than three or four minutes, without replying. A less patient man might have repeated his question, but Bingham was content to wait and watch.

The man's trousers were held up by braces – something Bingham had not seen worn, except on stage, for years – and they sagged open at the waist, as though the man had lost weight or was wearing someone else's clothes. His feet were bare and in his free hand – the one not supporting his body against the open door – he held a can of beer. His eyes peered out through black circles of fatigue and his teeth or what remained of them were turning from yellow to black.

The smell that followed him from the room was a unique blend of stale beer, rotten food and urine run through with something altogether sweeter. Despite it being only late afternoon, no light percolated into the room. The drawn curtains, Bingham decided, were probably never opened: a habit occasioned by laziness and subterfuge. This man lived hidden from the world, emerging only to buy what was needed to survive: food, alcohol and hash.

While Bingham watched and smelled, the man scrutinised him through tired eyes befuddled by the light of day. Eventually, after opening and closing his mouth several times in what seemed to be a vain attempt to speak, he said:

"What d'yer want?"

"May we speak inside … please?"

Bingham added the 'please', supposing it was a word the man rarely used and sensing that it would catch his attention. The man did smile the knowing smile of the uncouth, judging that courtesy implied weakness.

"What d'er want?"

"My name's George Bingham. I'm from the UK."

He didn't want to say anymore for fear the man might shut the door.

"You're English?"

"Yes."

"You can always tell."

"How's that?"

The man sniggered as though he thought that being English was a natural joke, and then, with a leer in his eyes, continued to stare at Bingham in silence. There was a degree of menace in the repetition of this pantomime, but the abiding feeling Bingham had was one of being bullied by a man who seldom found himself in a position of power over anyone. His smile never faltered as he waited.

"I said 'what do you want'," muttered the man, eventually.

"Are you Mr Paisley?"

"Let's suppose I am."

The change in the man's manner of speech was not lost on Bingham; it was a style that would be called 'posh' today, where slang infiltrated everywhere.

"Because of what I must ask you, let's suppose nothing. Are you Liam Paisley?"

"Who gave you my name?"

"I'm not prepared to say."

"Then I'm not prepared to listen. Good day."

It was unfortunate that the man added the farewell before he attempted to slam the door in Bingham's face because it alerted Bingham to his intention. As soon as the door moved towards him, Bingham's foot moved towards the door. He jammed it open and, not wanting a scene on the street, shoved it backwards, catching the man off-balance and propelling him into his own living room. Bingham stepped inside and closed the door gently behind him before drawing back the curtains and opening the windows.

"We might need to have a long chat, Mr Paisley – I assume it is Mr Paisley? – and the smell in here is rather unpleasant."

"What the fuck ..."

Liam Paisley said no more before lunging at Bingham with the half-empty beer can and stumbling onto his own floor as Bingham stepped aside.

Bingham watched him struggle to his feet and collapse onto a stained and tattered sofa, exhausted by his attack.

"You are Liam Paisley?"

"Yes."

"Is there anyone else in the house?"

A look of fear crossed Liam Paisley's eyes.

"What I want to discuss with you is private – that's why I ask," said Bingham, attempting to reassure the man, an attempt that turned out to be unnecessary.

The look had faded as quickly as it appeared; Liam Paisley was a man used to judging a threat and did not see one in Bingham.

"How long have you lived in Guaro?"

It was simple question, spoken to reassure and nothing more.

"Twenty years give or take a few."

"Since the late 90s?"

"About then."

"You must miss Ireland. It's a beautiful country."

"I've never lived there. Born and bred in Birmingham."

"You've never been to your homeland?"

"Once we visited an aunt of my mother's, but otherwise no. It costs a bit to travel and my mother never had the wherewithal."

"You were brought up by your mother?"

"Yes. My father buggered off soon after I was born. I don't remember him at all. He was just a stray sperm in the night – but they were married," he added, hastily, as though the idea of being born 'on the other side of the blanket' was an indecency he couldn't countenance.

"Are you married?"

"I was but ...," replied Liam Paisley, leaving the sentence unfinished and shrugging his shoulders, "Now, I use the brothels and there are plenty of those."

Looking at the man, Bingham wondered how often he was fit enough even to make it to a brothel.

Liam Paisley looked at him, as though reading Bingham's mind, and gave another shrug. A man holding on to what he once perceived as his manhood, which was now long gone. His eyes closed, weary with the tiredness of doing nothing. When he opened them again, there appeared in his look a realisation that he was talking to a stranger who had barged his way into his home.

"Who did you say you were?"

"My name's George Bingham."

"It means nothing to me."

"No."

"Who gave you my name?"

"This is where I came in," replied Bingham, with a smile, "I can't give you the name of the person, but I can explain why it was given to me."

Again, there was a long silence while Liam Paisley absorbed this information and tried to make some sense of what Bingham had said. There was a lack of uncertainty, which might have been expected, in his manner and a remembering of customs long forgotten.

"Can I offer you a drink?" he asked, after his lengthy consideration.

"Thank you," replied Bingham, who disliked intensely the modern habit of drinking from the can or the bottle, but on this occasion was pleased to do so.

"Would you help yourself? They're in the fridge."

There was no lack of manners in Liam Paisley's request: it was simply that he was incapable of lifting himself off the sofa. When Bingham returned from the kitchen, where the piles of food cartons adorned the draining board and spilled from the litter bin, he thought to himself that it was the first house in which he had ever set foot where there were no plates, mugs, cutlery or glasses visible. Did Liam Paisley live entirely from packets and cans, eating with his fingers?

The Irishman had not moved except to lift himself into a more upright sitting position. Bingham handed him another beer, and then cracked open his own can.

"Now, Mr Bingham, what can I do for you?"

Bingham had had time to consider how he was to approach his questioning of Liam Paisley. Experiences in Guaro del Mar had taught him that mention of the Mayhews' disappearance brought only evasion, antagonism or silence: in some instances, all three. He wasn't a natural liar, and Lina had insisted from the start of their relationship that even the smallest fib was not to be tolerated, but he felt that a certain edging in from the truth might be appropriate where this man was concerned.

"I work for a missing persons' agency," he lied, "It has nothing to do with the government: it is privately run, financed by people who want family members who have disappeared found. Such people, desperate for news of their loved ones, are prepared to pay for our services. Our rates are reasonable – we charge £200 a day plus expenses – and families are willing to pay for information."

Bingham's rigmarole was intended to achieve several ends: allay any fears Liam Paisley might harbour with regard to talking about the Mayhews, induce him to think there might be money to be made by cooperating and encourage him to believe that Bingham was simply a paid investigator and nothing more.

"How much would any information I might have be worth?"

"How much would you consider reasonable?"

"I think we'd be looking at ten grand."

"I think we might consider half that amount, but only if what you had to say led us to finding Colin and Patty Mayhew."

Bingham's mention of the missing couple brought the expected look of consternation in Paisley's face, a look that was replaced almost immediately by one of cunning.

"I didn't say I knew where they were."

"If that's the case I need bother you no further, Mr Paisley."

"I might be able to point you in the right direction."

"How did you come to meet Patty and Colin?"

"I didn't say I did … but I might have heard some gossip. Word gets around."

"They must have come to Spain at about the same time as you – twenty years ago, wasn't it?"

"It might have been."

"Things were easier, then?"

"Easier?"

"There was more money about – safer on the streets – that kind of thing."

"It was certainly safer on the streets."

Bingham could see that the man regretted making the comment as soon as it passed his lips. Fear was written in every twitch of his face and every changing expression in his eyes. Liam Paisley gulped, struggled from the sofa, and made his way to the windows Bingham had opened. He shut them with a slam and pulled the curtains back across.

The only light left in the room was that which peered through the gaps and tears. Bingham rose and turned on the overhead bulb that cast a faint, yellow glow. While there was light from the window, Bingham had minimal difficulty hearing Liam Paisley but with the curtains closed he was unable to read the man's lips. Suffering from encroaching deafness, he'd always found that a help; now, in the semi-darkness, he attached his hearing aids before continuing.

"Did you socialise with Colin and Patty?"

Liam Paisley laughed.

"We lived in different worlds."

"But you did know them?"

The man's reluctance to acknowledge any connection with the Mayhews was painful to watch; he was torn between his need for the money he supposed Bingham had to offer and his fear of reprisals.

There were many assumptions he could have made, but Bingham was reluctant to indulge in guesswork. There was no reason to suppose that the connection was even criminal; indeed, there was every chance that it was not. It wasn't even clear that Liam Paisley had any information worth offering, except for the fact that Lieutenant Palos had, however reluctantly, given Bingham his name. Why the reluctance and why had the policeman prised nothing from the man?

"How well did you know Colin and Patty?"

The use of the missing couple's Christian names was intended to evoke both sympathy and familiarity, although Bingham wondered whether he was wasting his time. Druggies like Paisley lived only for themselves. Bingham knew that from the few he'd met as a teacher during his working life.

"I came across them sometimes."

"Did you know any of their friends?"

"I said we moved in different circles."

"What was your business with them?"

"Business!"

"You had dealings with Colin and Patty."

It might have been inspiration on Bingham's part or merely a slip of the tongue. He'd meant business in the personal rather than the commercial sense but had hit some nail or other squarely on the head.

"Who told you that?"

"It doesn't matter who told me, but it's why I'm here," replied Bingham, and then added almost as an afterthought, "I'm after Colin and Patty's business associates."

"There was no association. I had nothing to do with it."

"But you did, Liam, you did, and now you can put matters right and help me find them."

"Put matters right!"

"You know what I mean."

Fear became terror in Liam Paisley's eyes. In the safety of his lounge he'd become a hunted animal. He felt the hounds on his heels and the knife in his guts.

"You don't know what you're up against. You've no idea."

"People keep telling me that but I'm still looking for the Mayhews and I won't stop until I find them. Your name came up as part of my search."

Bingham's eyes never left the other man's face and conveyed the impression he knew more than he did. The longer Liam Paisley jumped to conclusions the weaker became his position. Then, like a cornered rat, he turned.

"Give me a minute. I must …," he muttered.

An unhealthy, yellow sweat had broken out all over his face and the man began to chew his bottom lip. The trembling that had shaken his body and rattled his teeth ever since Bingham entered the house became a shudder and Liam Paisley's body seemed to be moving in several different directions at the same time.

Bingham watched the man skulk off to the kitchen, and assumed he was going for a fix of some kind. Bingham's knowledge of drug taking was academic. Once, at a friend's wedding, he'd seen a young couple slink off to the toilets and those around him had muttered about their taking drugs; but that was all he'd experienced at first hand.

When Liam Paisley returned, he sank, visibly relieved, once more onto the sofa. He handed Bingham another can of beer and opened one for himself.

"Ten years, or so, ago I used to go down to the harbour nearly every day. I was better then. That was when I got to know Colin. He had a boat, but he wasn't used to them and needed some help. He'd bought it, see, like a lot of people do when they retire, and he knew nothing about boats. Well, I knew Eusebio and the lads – I'd buy fish from them – and we soon got Colin used to handling his little cruiser. He was all right was Colin. Nice chap. I never really met his wife except occasionally when she'd come down to the boat and sit there drinking coffee. She didn't like the water, but she enjoyed being seen on the boat."

"Did you go out with him, like el Jefe?"

"You've spoken to Eusebio?"

"Yes."

"It wasn't him who gave you my name?"

"No. Go on. You were telling me about Colin."

"We'd go fishing – only with a line, but it was relaxing."

"Did he take drugs?"

"No. Not Colin. His missus would have gone nuts."

"But drugs were part of the trip?"

"No. You're on the wrong track Mr Bingham. You're floundering in deep water."

"Fish me out. Use the boathook."

The humour appealed to the Irishman who chuckled through a mouthful of beer until he choked and coughed up phlegm.

"You shouldn't make jokes like that, Mr Bingham. You shouldn't ..."

Bingham thought he saw a look of cunning mingle with the discomfort in the man's eyes but couldn't place the reason for it. He felt he was no nearer driving Liam Paisley to divulge anything of the truth than when he arrived.

"How long is it since you went down to the harbour regularly?"

"Why do you ask?"

"I was wondering how recently it was you'd seen Colin."

"How long before he disappeared, you mean?"

"Yes."

"I had nothing to do with that. I liked Colin. It wasn't my fault."

"How long was it, Liam?"

"You're on the wrong track."

"Each time we get close to an answer, we hear that phrase. How long was it before he disappeared that you and he met up?"

"Years."

"Really? You may have had nothing to do with his and Patty's disappearance, but you do know why they disappeared, don't you?"

"Get out."

"Not until you've earned your money. Who was it, Liam? Who was responsible for their disappearance? They didn't just run away, did they?"

"Perhaps they did. Perhaps they did just that – run away."

"Where would they have run to?"

"I don't know. I swear before God Almighty; I don't know where they are."

"But you liked Colin and you enjoyed watching Patty sitting on the boat drinking coffee. You must want to find out where they are just as much as we do."

"We?"

"I'm not alone: we work in pairs at the agency. My partner is an ex-policeman …"

Bingham's pause was deliberate: he wanted Liam Paisley to believe he knew more than he did.

"I can see that news has upset you just a little. Now, let us have the names of Colin's business associates."

"You knew I'd done time back in the UK."

"We might have done," Bingham lied.

"I wasn't always like this, you know."

"When did you first start on the drugs? Was it in prison?"

"Yes. Here, in Spain, I did three years for smuggling hash. But I'd never touched the stuff myself 'til I was nicked. There's nothing else to do in prison."

"How was Colin involved in this business?"

"I keep telling you – he wasn't … I've messed up so many times in my life. I'm lucky to be here at all."

The sudden switch in the man's line of thinking disturbed Bingham: he didn't want Liam Paisley veering off in another direction but felt that this time it might lead somewhere.

"You have friends who've covered your back at times?"

"Yes. How'd you know?"

Bingham didn't know any more than he had when his foot jammed open the door. Once again, his intuition had slipped into gear, or was it just another slip of the tongue?

"I sensed it," he replied.

"Do you know I speak fluent Spanish and a bit of Arabic – enough to get by. I was useful in Morocco in the old days."

"The old days – before the gangs from eastern Europe appeared on the scene?"

"Yes. You've hit the nail on the head, Mr Bingham. It was the hash that screwed me up. I could have had a normal family life. I was married once but she left me when I was in prison. You can't blame her. She could see the picture. She knew that even after I got out, I'd be in the hands of the gangs. You're always watching your back, you see. One false move and you've had it. You can't live like that – not for long – and it wasn't what she wanted; God bless her."

"Were there any children?"

"A boy. I haven't seen him – ever. He was born soon after I went to prison. When I came out, she'd gone."

"And you've no idea where?"

"Home – well out of the way."

"Where's home?"

"Serbia. She was lured here on the promise of dancing in the clubs but, of course, most of them end up in the brothels. She was lucky – she met me just in time. I suppose that's one good thing I've done."

Liam Paisley laughed a hard laugh, a laugh devoid of any suggestion of mirth, but Bingham realized that he saw the woman as his one good deed in life. In its way this belief was a comfort and a kind of salvation.

"Have you had any run-ins with the police since you came out of prison?"

"No. I got involved in the coke business. That's why they nabbed me."

"You said you went to prison for smuggling hash."

"They couldn't prove – or didn't want to prove – my connection with the coke trade. So, they got me for the hash. They normally tend to turn a blind eye to hash, especially if we grease their palms."

"We?"

"Careful, Mr Bingham," replied Liam Paisley, the shifty look returning to his eyes, "You don't need to know too much."

"You've never used coke yourself?"

"No."

A shiver of apprehension – no more, but enough to frighten him – passed along Bingham's spine. He was averse to jumping too quickly to conclusions, and Bingham did wonder whether, this time, he had broken his golden rule. Was Liam Paisley's explanation leading him nowhere? Despite having spent the best part of an afternoon with the man, he was no further forward. All he had was what he and Brockie already knew: in various ways many of these locals were mixed up in the drugs trade.

"You'll get nothing more from me, Mr Bingham. It's too dangerous. You can forget your five grand. I'd rather stay alive."

Liam Paisley had strung him along, revealing nothing: no names, no connections and no way forward. Moreover, the man had read his mind, taking him for a fool. Bingham stood up from the chair on which he'd squatted, wondering whether he should have brought Brockie with him. He nodded to Liam Paisley who still lolled, smirking, on the tatty sofa.

Bingham opened the door and left, making his way along various back streets towards the harbour, wondering where Brockie had ended up after his interview with Jorge Demara and whether his friend had been more successful.

"Mr Bingham?"

It was a question and Bingham thought he recognised the voice. He wondered why, since normally he heard nothing spoken from behind, and then realised he was still wearing his hearing aids.

As he turned to answer, something struck him in the face with such force that tears sprung from his eyes and he cried out in pain. Before he could open his eyes and look, another blow, delivered with brutal precision to his stomach, took Bingham's breath away. His legs were kicked from under him and he fell to the pavement. A barrage of blows followed, some aimed at his back and others at his stomach. He couldn't decide whether he was being struck with feet or fists.

The pain was intolerable, and he feared for his bones: old and frail they might easily be broken. Someone stood on his hand that was outstretched on the pavement and ground it into the stones. Bingham screamed again, aware for the first time in his life how awful it was to have others free to inflict whatever pain they fancied on your body.

Finally, someone lifted his head from the ground by twisting a hand in his mop of hair and yanking his face upwards, although not far enough for Bingham to identify the speaker.

"You're a lucky man, Mr Bingham. You could be on your way to the hills. Go home."

His head was thrust back onto the pavement, another kick was delivered to his ribs and Bingham was left alone, blood seeping from somewhere and his breathing painful to endure.

Chapter Seven
A SENSE OF DECENCY

When he regained consciousness, Bingham found himself in a hospital bed. Brockie and Lieutenant Palos were watching him.

"Are you all right, George?" asked Brockie, when Bingham's eyes rested on his friend.

"Sparkling," he replied, with a grin at his friend's humour.

He could feel the bruising on his face and the swellings round his eyes simply by the effort of trying to twitch his cheeks. Bingham ran his tongue around the inside of his mouth and found his teeth intact. He was relieved. The pain in his side and back was just about bearable, although he found both breathing and stretching difficult. His abdomen throbbed persistently with a sharp discomfort rather like an empty socket when a tooth has been extracted. Looking at his body, Bingham realized his right hand was bound and plastered.

"Are there any broken bones?" he asked.

"Possibly a small rib fracture that will mend itself naturally in time," said Brockie, "but the fingers of your right hand are rather more severely damaged, of course."

"Of course. How did I get here?"

"A young man brought you in. You were conscious but kept passing out. He left after telling the medical people to phone the police."

"You've no idea who he was?"

"No," replied Lieutenant Palos, barely meeting Bingham's gaze.

The policeman was in uniform, and so smart he might have been attending an investiture or going on parade. His hair was immaculately coiffured, and his little moustache waxed and trimmed to perfection. His face shone and his small mouth seemed pursed to receive either a kiss or a cigarette. Bingham wondered whether he'd been preparing himself to dine out for the evening when the call came from the medical centre.

"Have you any idea who did this to you, George?"

"No, but I'm sure we can find out rather quickly," replied Bingham, his eyes never leaving the policeman's face. "Lieutenant, have you obtained a description of the young man?"

"Yes."

"Is he known to you?"

"We're looking into the matter, Mr Bingham. I'm sure we'll find him."

"Is there any chance you could hurry proceedings along, Lieutenant? Time is of the essence. I'd be most grateful. You see, I have an idea who the young man might be. If we could find him, we may trace the men who attacked me more easily."

"I don't quite understand what you mean, Mr Bingham."

"Neither do I, but I'm sure the description given by the medical people would help. There's no chance, is there, that you could fetch it for me?"

The eyebrows were raised but slightly and the smooth skin of his face stretched as Lieutenant Palos widened his eyes in controlled surprise. He wasn't a man to be flustered any more than he was a man to be ordered about by an Englishmen, however politely.

"I think we could manage that, Mr Bingham," he replied, turning on his heels and leaving the room.

Did he hear a click as the heels met, wondered Bingham? No, it was his imagination.

"Brockie, would you be kind enough to pass my jacket? Thank you."

Bingham ferreted in one of his pockets, found the slip of paper he was seeking and handed it to his friend.

"Would you go to this address? I'm anticipating you'll find a mobile phone somewhere in the house. Pocket it and bring it here, will you? No time for questions, Brockie. Take no nonsense from the householder and avoid the lieutenant on your way out. Thanks. I know this goes against the grain. I appreciate it. Oh, and be careful."

Bingham smiled at his friend but relieved the frown on Brockie's face only slightly.

Two surprises awaited Lieutenant Palos when he returned: Bingham was struggling into his clothes and there was no sign of his friend. Bingham read both anxieties in the Spaniard's face and amused himself by wondering which concerned the policeman most.

"Don't worry about Brockie, Lieutenant. He is pursuing our investigation with some vigour but can look after himself. I think you and I have some talking to do."

"You're not thinking of leaving here, Mr Bingham?"

"That's why I'm nearly dressed. I was hoping you might give me a lift back to the La Fonda. I'd much rather talk there, and I also feel rather peckish … I'm not dragging you away from a dinner date, am I?"

"No, no. I shall be only too pleased to return you to your hotel."

"Do you have the description of the young man?"

"Certainly! One of my officers has produced a sketch."

"Jet black hair, curling round his ears?"

"You know this man?"

"Yes. He's only a boy really. What I don't know is why he happened to find me on the pavement. We need to talk, Lieutenant."

Back at the La Fonda, a table was cleared and prepared rapidly when the hotel staff realised the state of their guest and the presence of an officer of the Guardia Civil.

The menu was extensive, but Bingham always ate local produce when he could and so chose sardines en escabeche. The waiter was pleased to explain that this was "an Arabian dish", and Bingham thought how appropriate that was since he'd spent the afternoon with an Irishman who spoke Arabic. He smiled to himself as Lieutenant Palos insisted upon ordering the wine.

"Delicately fruity," explained the policeman, "with just a prickle in the mouth – perfect with fish."

The case was closing in, thought Bingham – 'the end was nigh'. He wasn't sure why he felt so optimistic, considering his bruised body. Perhaps it was the policeman's discomfort; perhaps it was the fact that he knew the young man; perhaps it because Brockie was, probably at this very moment, disturbing the evening of a man he had no reason to trust. He and his friend had only been in Guaro del Mar for two days, but they were disturbing people, stirring the pond, shaking the dust, troubling the waters.

"Cheers, Lieutenant," he said with a smile as he took his first gulp of wine that evening. "Would you prefer to discuss this matter during the meal or wait until we have completed our repast?"

Bingham enjoyed old-fashioned phrases: they connected him with another world, a world where language held sway.

"Perhaps it would be more relaxing to talk after we've dined, but at least allow me to apologise for what happened to you, Mr Bingham. I cannot express, adequately, how distressed and responsible I feel."

"Apologies accepted, Lieutenant. Let's enjoy our meal."

The fish fell easily apart in Bingham's mouth and he eventually made his way slowly through a baked caramel custard accompanied by a cream sherry. After his apology, the policeman relaxed. He chatted generally, leaving Bingham to concentrate on the now difficult task of eating.

They found a quiet corner after the meal and Bingham waited patiently while the policeman gathered his words.

"Let me begin by saying, Mr Bingham, that I had no idea you would be subjected to a beating when I gave you Paisley's address, but … I must confess I hesitated and, therefore, at the back of my mind I must have anticipated the possibility, however remote, of such a thing happening. For that, I can only offer, once again, my sincere apologies."

Bingham had noted the pause, which he put down to official discretion. He liked the policeman but didn't altogether trust him, and so he smiled, nodded and waited.

"We had discovered nothing from Paisley during our investigation into Senor and Senora Mayhew's disappearance, and I had hoped you might gain some information for us. I had noticed certain qualities in you – patience, wisdom, a quiet disposition – and thought Paisley might be encouraged to talk as he would not do with an official such as myself."

Bingham didn't smile at the flattery. He didn't like being buttered up, and his opinion of the policeman took a downward step.

"What linked Senor Paisley to the possible fate of the Mayhews?"

"You are very direct, Mr Bingham."

"I'm tired, I ache all over and I've had a long day."

"I assure you that we do not know what happened to Senor and Senora Mayhew."

"But it is clear they were abducted, isn't it? No one invites guests to dinner and then decide to run away while the rabbit is being stewed. Crime in Guaro del Mar centres around the drugs trade and even though nothing has been found to link the Mayhews with drugs there is the strong possibility that a connection exists."

"The Mayhews had few friends outside their own circle, but one of them was Senor Paisley. Did you find out anything from him?"

Bingham relayed the substance of his conversation with the drug addict, eased himself to a more comfortable position in his chair for the umpteenth time and waited. Liam Paisley had run circles round him. He hadn't expected to do the talking; he was waiting for an explanation.

"His wife was the link we wanted," continued the policeman, "We knew about her, naturally. She was lucky on two counts: she was Serbian, and Paisley married her. Girls are brought here from all over the world – South American, England, Scotland, Serbia, Romania, Albania, Russia … I could go on. They are lured by the promise of work as barmaids, dancers, waitresses, singers in the nightclubs, but many end up in the brothels of the Costa.

Paisley had lived here for many years when she came, and we had reason to suppose that he met her through his work – work that connected him to one of the many Serbian gangs. Because he knew the Mayhews, Senor Paisley was our one link between them and the gangsters, and – if they were abducted – it would be one of these gangs who were responsible … Paisley gave you no idea of his wife's family connections?"

"No. He merely said that she had returned home with their child when he went to prison for smuggling hash."

"She was probably sent home."

"Which of these gangs were involved with Paisley's smuggling activities?"

"We never found out. These people never talk."

Fear was the key to the mystery of the English couple's disappearance. Bingham had decided that on his first day, which was less than forty-eight hours ago but seemed to stretch back years. No one would say more than necessary to save their own skin, and sometimes not as much. If Liam Paisley was the link between the Mayhews and their fate, he was a tenuous one.

"My beating was a warning, Lieutenant – I assume you have already drawn that conclusion. Since these gangs are ruthless, I think we can dismiss the idea of them having any part in the attack. They would simply have killed me. Only two people knew where I was this afternoon, only these two people could have arranged the beating to urge me to return home: Liam Paisley and you."

Had Bingham slapped him round the face, the policeman could not have been more offended and mortified. The expression on his face suggested that he was on the verge of challenging Bingham to a duel, and that only Bingham's injuries were restraining him.

"You are all frightened, aren't you? You, Jorge Demara, Senor Garcas, Fred Jackson alias Patrick Sims, Eusebio Abad and his friends, Liam Paisley … need I go on? All of you want Brockie and me out of the way."

"I find your words insulting in the extreme, Mr Bingham."

"I don't blame you. If I lived here I would be terrified most of the time – *if I were in any way connected with these gangs* either through my work, like you, my position, like Senor Demara and Senor Garcas, or my criminal activities, like the others I have mentioned. It seems to me that what I will call the normal residents of Guaro del Mar have far less to fear, if anything at all, *unless they are unfortunate enough to be in the way at a critical moment*. Am I right?"

"There is some truth in what you say."

"And so, we have to decide whether the Mayhews were simply unfortunate or whether they were criminals – and rather clever ones since, if they were, they kept their activities a secret even from you."

The Spaniard was flattered by the compliment but not mollified; his anger at Bingham's unintended insult showed in his eyes.

"I was merely outlining the possibilities, Lieutenant. When I embarked on my first investigation, a real detective – a very painstaking one, my friend Simon

Brockie – told me that 'the art of investigation is to explore possibilities, confirm the negatives and eliminate all explanations of what might have happened until only one remains', and that is what I am doing. If Brockie has been successful tonight, we should know within a short time who was responsible for giving me this beating. You might care to join us for breakfast tomorrow morning. We've found a nice little café on the waterfront."

Their parting was just civil, no more, and Bingham regretted his rudeness, but only slightly. At the centre of this investigation was an elderly couple – content in their own company, devoted to each other, "always locked in each other's arms" – who had disappeared without trace and who, one way or another, needed to be found.

Bingham was surprised that Brockie had not returned during the meal but, at the same time, relieved. He had another mission that night, one he wanted to tackle alone, unimpeded by objections from his friend. He waited until the policeman was well clear of the hotel, asked for a walking stick at the reception desk and went outside where taxis were always waiting.

It was by pure chance that he came across the very taxi driver who had shown them the way to the Mayhews' villa on their first morning. He had no reason to trust the man but decided he had no reason to trust anybody, and he wanted a word with this one. Bingham instructed him to drive to the corner of the Calle Calvario, where he struggled from the taxi and leaned in at the open window where the man waited for his payment.

"I believe you're the gentleman who showed my friend and me to the home of Senor and Senora Mayhew."

The driver nodded and, once again, threw Bingham a broad smile, removed a cigarette from between a set of jagged white teeth and chuckled.

"You then took the trouble to send Senor Jackson after us. Perhaps you were concerned that my friend and I might get lost – hmm?"

The smile faded, the cigarette drooped and hung from the driver's bottom lip.

"I won't be getting lost tonight, my friend, and should I find I am followed I might persuade Lieutenant Palos to ask a few questions about your licence. Do you understand me?"

Bingham had wanted the Spanish word for 'revoke', feeling it might have had a greater effect, but his vocabulary was more of the street than the office.

He couldn't decide whether the driver's look was one of anger, fear, dislike or a blend of all three as the man yanked his steering wheel across and screeched off.

Bingham knew his way from the corner of Calle Calvario and was soon stumbling, sweat damping his shirt collar, through the narrow streets and small plazas of the old town. Occasionally he stopped, waited and listened but heard no footsteps behind, only the natural sounds of the night: chatter from the open windows, children called to bed, families clearing the evening meal. He found the café he sought easily and sat at the very table where he'd waited for Richard Brown only that morning. The patroness recognised him and smiled.

"Do you have a glass of the Alberino," he said, having enjoyed the lieutenant's recommendation earlier.

When she placed the wine before him, accompanied by the olives and small rolls, the woman asked about his wounds. There was more than sympathy in her voice:

there was concern and outrage that a visitor to her town should have been assaulted.

"I was left on the pavement," replied Bingham, "but the young man found me and took me to the hospital. I've come to thank him. Is it possible you could get a message to Senor Brown?"

The woman's expression changed, but only slightly; outrage was suddenly mixed with anxiety and doubt as she struggled to her decision.

"You seemed to know him well," continued Bingham, "I remember you placing his cola before him without asking what he wanted. I'd hoped you might know where he lives."

She called to one of the children who were still running around the plaza, splashing their hands in and out of the fountain, cooling themselves in the heat of the night.

"Lupila! See if you can find Ricardo. Tell him his friend of the morning is here."

The little girl, her light dress lifting as she ran, hurried off along one of the narrow passageways, as safe as houses thought Bingham and felt relieved that he was among ordinary people in this dangerous town.

When he arrived, Richard Brown took Bingham's outstretched left hand and received his thanks with a cautious smile. The patroness placed a large cola in front of him.

"How did you know it was me?"

"I recognised the sketch the police made from the description given by the hospital staff."

"Do the Guardia know you're here?"

"No one knows I'm here. I came to thank you and ask for your further help."

"Go home, Mr Bingham."

"I can't do that until I've found out what happened to the Mayhews. Can you tell me how it was you happened to be passing my way this afternoon?"

"I have a customer on that rundown estate."

"Liam Paisley?"

"No, but you're close. There're several deadbeats hanging out there. Had you been talking to Paisley?"

"Yes. Help me, Richard. You cared enough to carry me to that medical centre. Care enough to …"

"Don't tell me what to care about, Mr Bingham – you haven't lived my life. You won't have to stay alive here once … once this is over."

"Liam Paisley had a Serbian wife."

"I know all about her. They sent her home after the police nabbed Paisley. Guaro's no place for an attractive woman on her own with a child. One of the gangs would soon find her work."

"If the Mayhews were linked to this gang, Paisley was that link, wasn't he?"

"That's a big 'if', Mr Bingham."

"I don't think so, and neither do you. Do you know where I might find this particular gang?"

"I take it the police don't know," returned Richard Brown, with a smile, "Ever wondered why?"

"Do you know?"

"Everyone knows, but no one's saying."

"I imagine Liam Paisley talks when he's drunk."

"What do you mean?"

"Nothing … but I might have to pay him another visit. He should be well gone by now. He was sozzled when I left him … just before I was beaten up this afternoon."

The patroness was approaching their table with another cola and a bottle of the Alberino to top up Bingham's glass as he spoke but paused as she felt the tension between the two men. Bingham drained his glass and felt for his wallet. He eased himself back from the table and stood, pain showing in his every move.

"Bugger you," said the young man, "Leave it with me but don't call me, I'll call you."

He threw a glance at the patroness, and then stormed off across the plaza. Bingham smiled as he left his payment on the table. He turned to the woman and thanked her.

"A nice young man; a decent young man," he said, wondering whether he'd tapped wrongly into that sense of decency, that feeling for right and wrong men like Richard Brown possessed, a feeling that required a conscience.

It had been a long, painful day but Bingham had just one more thing to do before he could sleep. He made his way back to the la Fonda, hoping to find Brockie in possession of a stolen mobile phone.

The next morning, they sat together in the café frequented by Eusebio Abad and his friends, the café where the waitress had been kind and the patron's wife concerned for Bingham's safety. Brockie, intolerant of foreign food and essentially British, ordered poached eggs on toast but Bingham, who always ate in the local style, enjoyed café con leche, zumo and tostadas. They were joined by Lieutenant Palos and the mobile phone was placed on the table between them.

Once again, Bingham was delighted by the stillness of the morning: the sky, the boats, the tourists, the fishermen and the sea. Even the water lapped quietly against the harbour wall and the pontoons. Bingham enjoyed the sound of the ropes tap-tap-tapping the masts of the yachts, the occasional, almost apologetic, roar of an outboard motor, the sound of an oar sliding in the rowlocks.

The three men ate quietly, Brockie and Bingham slightly tense at what the outcome of their scheme might be, wondering whether the lieutenant already knew and had made his preparations. The young waitress was missing, much to Bingham's disappointment, and her place was taken by a youth who seemed to be the son of the owners. The patron's wife had greeted Bingham and his friend, her face still anxious.

Bingham was normally a fast eater but had paced himself that morning, partly because the peaceful atmosphere demanded he should, partly because he now found eating difficult, partly because he was waiting for Eusebio Abad and his friends to appear on the quayside. When they did, he allowed them to greet each other and settle to their early chat and then nodded to Brockie.

"I think it's time for Mr Paisley's 4.30 call, Simon. If we're right, you may need reinforcements, Lieutenant."

It would, of course, have been far easier to have asked the policeman to check the owner of the number Liam Paisley had rung on his mobile phone sometime around 4.30 the previous afternoon but Bingham enjoyed a touch of the dramatic and he knew that someone, somewhere, was going to answer the call. He rather hoped it would be el Jefe.

He was not disappointed. Brockie had no sooner tapped in the number than the fisherman reached for his phone. Bingham rose, resting heavily on his walking stick, and ambled across to the group of men, the ones he had dubbed 'the rats of the waterfront'. Eusebio Abad was still waiting for Liam Paisley to speak when Bingham reached him.

The group of men looked at Bingham, the expressions on their faces a sullen mix of puzzlement and dislike. It was strange to think that only the previous evening at least some of them must have kicked and punched him to the ground. There was violence in them: in the scowl of their faces, the manner of their standing, the clench of their fists, the strut of their crotches and the tension in their shoulders.

Bingham wondered what they were thinking as they gazed at him. The bruises on his body were hidden but the swellings on his face had now darkened to the purple colour of early bruising and the binding on his right hand was clear for all to see.

"Which of you was it who stood on my hand?" he asked.

They didn't have to answer and there was no point in their adopting expressions of dumb ignorance. He'd seen it all before in the louts he'd dealt with as a teacher: the more amazed the expression, the more likely the guilt. Bingham's cold eye fell on his man. He was one of those who'd been wearing a blue serge jacket on that first morning, the one who had preferred a cigar when they came to the café.

"There was no need for that little extra touch of cruelty," he said, "The beating was warning enough."

Bingham had made no decision as to what he would do when he approached the fishermen. It may well have been enough to eye them over and return for another coffee. Normally a placid man, he was given, at times, to sudden impulses. Perhaps it was the fact that while most of his comrades were leaning on el Jefe's boat this one man was propped against a mooring post, his back to the open water; perhaps it was the arrogance of the man's expression. Bingham was as unsure of his motive as those others who watched were surprised. Quite suddenly, he half-fell half-slumped forward as though about to collapse and then raised his stick and shoved the fisherman hard in the chest. The man toppled backwards, caught his neck on one of the mooring ropes and hit the water with a huge splash.

Bingham watched him for a while and heard him scream. He couldn't swim. It didn't surprise Bingham: one of his uncles who had served in the submarine service during World War Two couldn't swim either. Bingham had learned that fact as a boy, surprised on his uncle's knee that sailors couldn't swim.

El Jefe's comrades rushed to help the man, while Lieutenant Palos seized his chance, signalled two of his men forward and took Eusebio Abad in for questioning. By the time the finger crusher was hauled ashore, his designer jeans and serge jacket a sodden mess, Bingham had re-joined Brockie at their breakfast table and was ordering another coffee.

Lieutenant Palos walked over to the men, had a few words with them and returned to Bingham's table.

"As you see, Senor Bingham, I had anticipated what you might have in mind, although not the manner of it. I've told Abad's men to stay at hand today since I may want to question them. The same applies to you. Do not leave the town. We may be obliged to charge you with assault."

The policeman turned on his heels and marched off to interrogate el Jefe, signalling the sodden man to follow him.

"A tap on the wrist for you, George."

"I suppose the Lieutenant was obliged to say something."

"The gentleman may well decide to press charges. You did assault him in front of witnesses. We must hope that the Lieutenant gets something useful out of these fishermen to make your imprisonment worthwhile."

"In the meantime, Brockie, we have a name – Ralko Devich. You say that Liam Paisley was terrified?"

"Had he not been as drunk as a lord, I wouldn't have got anything from him. But, as I said last night, he admitted the link between the Mayhews and this gang, although I'm not sure what the nature of that link was. We need to proceed carefully, George. Back home, I'd reel these characters in for questioning but out here that's just as likely to get us a bullet in the back as it is to get us answers."

Chapter Eight
THE GARDENER'S WIFE

At a loss as to how they might make headway with their investigation, Bingham and Brockie wandered off into the town, each man sharing his thoughts piecemeal with the other. Bingham knew from the late-night conversation they'd had when he returned to the La Fonda that Brockie had spoken with Lieutenant Palos on his return from Liam Paisley's house, omitting to mention the phone but enquiring about Ralko Devich.

The man was known to the Guardia. He was to all intents and purposes a "respectable businessman". He owned several bars and nightclubs as well as one of the more lucrative casinos. He also employed many local people in his businesses, including fifteen to twenty Brits who had retired to Spain. His clubs were known as being "clean" places, whereas many in the town were simply fronts for brothels.

He'd been mentioned in connection with the kidnapping of the girlfriend of a rival club owner, the random shooting of a local hash dealer in a night club, the "leaving out to dry" of a colleague who had been seen talking to the police and the slicing up of a Chinese gangster; but no charges had been brought due to a lack of eyewitness evidence.

Bingham's wounds were exhausting him and after a short while he suggested to Brockie that he needed to rest. They were sitting on a stone bench above a rainwater drain when Brockie noticed the woman approaching. He pointed her out to Bingham, who recognised her at once as the wife of the patron of the waterfront café where they'd had lunch: the woman who'd whispered her concerns for his safety in the privacy of her kitchen.

"Senores," she said, again in a hushed voice, "I must speak with you."

Bingham rose to greet the woman and asked her name, which she gave as Felipa Lamora. Bingham introduced himself and Brockie and began to explain why they had come to Guaro del Mar, but she cut him short.

"I know, senor. I know why you have come. There is much talk. I am at the market and so time is mine, but I must not linger."

Bingham thought it was the politest way in which he'd ever been told to stop talking.

"The men who hurt you are foolish rather than bad. They want you to go home before there is more trouble. I have heard them talking. Tonight, they were expected to have their boat out at sea. A cargo is coming. If they are not at the rendezvous, there will be trouble. The men they work for are evil. They will come ...," she said, crossing herself as she spoke the word 'evil' and pausing as though there was no word to describe what they might do.

"Who are these men?"

"They are the gangsters – the Serbians."

"Have you ever heard the name 'Ralko Devich'?"

"I know no names. I am warning you for your own safety. You will not find the people you seek. Only trouble can come from what you have done. El Jefe must be released. Do you understand? For your own safety – go!"

They received nothing more than a blessing from her. Senora Lamora turned and walked quickly away towards the market where she would find the produce to cook the wonderful meals her customers would enjoy that evening. She wanted them to be among that number; of that, Bingham had no doubt. He relayed what she had said to Brockie.

"There wouldn't be more than one such gang operating in this area of the town," said Brockie, "I'd bet a penny to a pound that this is the one we need to meet."

"Is Palos to be trusted?"

"If only there was no doubt about him, we might be seeing the light."

What both men were thinking involved the cooperation of others. If they were to lay these gangsters by the heels, they might have a chance of discovering what had become of Colin and Patty Mayhew. They might not, of course: the men, even if captured, might choose to remain silent. Bingham did not like uncertainties. He was adept at laying bare the bottom line of any enterprise, but he liked to be at the helm.

"If I might borrow your com … notepad, George, I'll contact various people I knew in the force. It'll take a while. What will you do?"

"I'll make my way to the Mayhews' villa. Don't ask me why … Oh, Brockie, if you think you have the clear on Palos, go ahead. This is your field rather than mine. I'm out of my depth."

"And if I don't?"

"Then our only hope lies in Richard Brown coming up with something. Good luck."

Bingham sat for a while after his friend had disappeared in the maze of narrow streets. His wounds were beginning to tell: the nagging pains were setting in, particularly in his useless right hand. All he really wanted was to sit quietly.

It was with this thought in mind that he arrived eventually at the Mayhews' villa. He hadn't expected to see anybody and wasn't disappointed. He sat on the patio, resting his most badly bruised leg on one chair and easing his back into another. A coffee would be welcome, he thought, wishing he were at home checking his hives, waiting for Lina to ring the dining bell, waiting for Pippa to share his snack.

The young woman appeared almost from nowhere, making her way up the hill towards the other villas. Although they'd never met, he knew her at once. It was Betran Julio's wife, cleaner of the English villas. She was an exceptionally beautiful young woman and her working clothes – the dark blue dress covered by the clean, white apron – seemed to add to the attraction. Her long, black hair was restrained by a headscarf that she seemed to have managed to tie without disturbing the flow of the hair. She was plump but petite. Bingham sensed her homeliness before she spoke.

"Senor and Senora Mayhew are not at home," she said, with a slight frown.

"I know. I met your husband two – or was it three – days ago."

"You are Senor Bingham?"

"Yes," he replied, struggling to lift his outstretched leg from the chair so that he could stand and greet the young woman, "I've been wounded. I just wanted to sit and rest."

"Please, there is no need to move, senor," she said with a laugh at his old-fashioned courtesy, "Would you like me to make you a coffee?"

"That would be wonderful," replied Bingham, supposing his prayer to have been answered by a Spanish angel.

She let herself into the Mayhews' villa and after a while returned with two cups of black coffee, the percolator and a plate of what looked like English biscuits.

"Senor and Senora Mayhew would not mind. They were kind people, very much in love in the Spanish way. Oh, my name is Camila," she said, holding out her hand to Bingham as she sat opposite him across the steel table.

"George," he replied, taking his first sip of coffee, "Did you know them well?

"Yes, I have always been cleaner here."

"I've only seen a photograph of them. It's strange to be drinking the coffee of someone you've never met … and sad to think they may never return to their home."

The silence that followed his remark was not uncomfortable. Bingham's movements were as self-effacing as his manner: he sat quietly, dunking a biscuit, waiting. When Camila Julio said nothing, he continued in the same tone.

"Your husband said you shopped for them."

"I shop for many of the ladies. I have friends at the market. I get a good price."

"You brought Patty Mayhew the rabbit she was cooking on the night she disappeared."

"Yes – and the onions, the chillies, the herbs, the tomatoes, the cucumber and the arugula, the oranges, all fresh from the market," she laughed, "I did not bring so much for all the ladies but Senor and Senora Mayhew were kind – especially kind."

It was the last phrase that caught Bingham's attention. He looked up at Camila Julio, realising they were speaking in English, and smiled.

"Your English is very good."

"As good as your Spanish, Senor Bingham? Betran was impressed."

"Better – and, please, call me George. You spoke with Patty Mayhew a good deal?"

"Yes, we would often talk. All the time I was cleaning we would talk. Sometimes the cleaning was done by Senora Mayhew before I arrived, and we would just sit and talk. It was good for me."

Camila poured Bingham another cup of coffee, dark brown and as thick as syrup. He refrained from broaching the question he wanted to ask.

"Patty Mayhew was looking forward to cooking for her friends."

"She always looked forward to her friends coming. On the morning, she would talk with me about Spanish cooking. It was me who gave her the recipe for the salmorejo."

"Stew," said Bingham.

"A very special stew."

"Did you and your husband ever eat with the Mayhews?"

"It was not considered ... it did not happen often, but after the storm of two winters ago, they came to our little house."

"After the storm?"

"The winds can be very bad in some years. Our roof was destroyed. Senor Mayhew insisted on paying for the repairs. He was truly kind. Betran and I wanted to thank him. We have only a small house, but it is important to us."

Bingham's mind went back to a moment during his first investigation – a moment he'd missed at the time, but which returned in the early hours of one morning when he could not sleep. Perhaps there were always such moments for the professionals. He didn't know, but this was another for him: the moment of a sudden insight, a quickening of understanding, the instant when a mystery is on the point of being solved.

"No house can be without a roof," he said, smiling, "There must have been much damage."

"Yes, and we had no insurance. It is too much to find ..."

Camila Julio's memory drifted back three years. Bingham watched her picturing their house without a roof; he saw the anguish in her face.

"When the roof was done," she continued, dreamily, "Senor Mayhew had the upstairs extended: only a small room but enough when the time comes."

She blushed and looked down at her feet.

"You are waiting for children?"

"They will come, and when they do, we have the extra room."

She could be one of my own daughters, thought Bingham, watching the young woman. Fiorenza does not even look like having a child and Cecilia – well there was Bruno, of course, but he'd not been intended. Bingham reached across the table and patted Camila's hand.

"You will be a good mother," he said, "I can see it in your eyes."

"I must go. I must go. I have work to do."

"Thank you for the coffee."

Bingham watched her clearing away the coffee things, locking the villa and waving to him as she walked up the hill to her cleaning job. Camila Julio hadn't asked whether he thought he might find the Mayhews. Perhaps she already guessed or knew the answer, as did many others who lived in Guaro del Mar.

As perhaps did Richard Brown, who found Bingham at the café run by Imelda Jackson where Bingham arranged to meet Brockie for lunch.

Bingham had made his way slowly there, hoping to quiz Fred Jackson but finding only his wife. Still hot and busy, Imelda Jackson placed a local beer in front of Bingham without being asked and welcomed him cheerfully as before. Bingham noted, again, the neatness of the place and thought he might as well settle there for lunch since all he could do was bide his time.

Richard Brown arrived soon after they'd finished their meal and before they'd shared their experiences of the morning. Brockie enjoyed guinea fowl in a nut sauce while Bingham, whose appetite had gone, settled for a bowl of gazpacho.

"Your friend?" snapped the young man, eyeing Brockie.

Bingham signalled to Imelda and ordered the young drug dealer a cola which brought a smile to his face.

"Yes. Simon Brockie – Richard Brown. You can speak freely in front of my friend, Richard. We're both here for the same reason. Can you help us?"

"I've got the names you wanted – or, more exactly, two names. Josif Bolich and Lazar Mudry. You won't forget them in a hurry should you ever meet, but I'll advise you again for the last time – go home."

The young man had leaned closer to Bingham when he spoke the names, but even so Bingham had difficulty hearing him so low was his voice. He wrote the names in his notebook and showed Richard Brown, who nodded.

"Why those two?" asked Bingham.

"*If* the Mayhews were involved with these gangsters, and *if* they fell out for some reason these two are the ones who would be most likely to sort things out."

"Does the name Ralko Devich mean anything to you?"

"For God's sake, Mr Bingham …"

"He's their leader, isn't he?"

"He's a respectable businessman. Let's leave it at that shall we?"

"What more can you tell us about the other two?"

The hesitation was painful to watch. Bingham had witnessed similar struggles in many a youth confessing to a misdemeanour, wriggling and screwing against his conscience and the fear of an imagined reprisal. Bingham smiled: at the worst, in the old days, it would have been a caning and, in what were described as 'more enlightened times', reference to a counsellor. Bingham knew which option he'd have chosen but might have gone for the counsellor if the other option had been assassination, which was the dilemma that faced Richard Brown.

"Richard," he said, "you've obtained this information because you were angry at my beating and felt genuine concern for the fate of the Mayhews. You're a decent young man despite your way of life. Complete the job."

"The gang are expecting a drop-off tonight. The two I mentioned are responsible for organising the safe house – as you might call it," added Richard Brown with a smile. "They've rented a place near one of the beaches. It's there that they'll store the hash while it's broken up for distribution. Once that's done the stuff will be repacked into smaller containers and make its way up through Spain and then France to Amsterdam unless it's going to be distributed locally through someone like me."

"Have you ever worked for these people?" asked Bingham.

"Don't be daft, Mr Bingham. I wouldn't be speaking to you like this if I had. They'd top me. Anyway, let me finish. The two I mentioned will be at this place near the beach tonight. If you and your friend are stupid enough to want to have a chat with them, you know where to go."

"Where did you get this information, sonny?" asked Brockie.

"Don't 'sonny' me, mate."

"It's just my friend's way of speaking, Richard. He meant no offence."

"Right, then I'll let it pass."

"Where did you find this out?" said Bingham, gazing steadily at the young man.

"Bloody hell, Mr Bingham, you don't half push it. I had a word with Liam Paisley, but you must have guessed that."

"I got nothing from him," said Brockie, "except the one name."

"Well, I was probably a bit more persuasive."

"You threatened him?"

"Just a little. Paisley's a lowlife. He'd sell his mother – if he had one – for a joint. Besides, he arranged your beating and that was out of order. I didn't hurt him too much."

"Is he likely to pass on what he's said?"

"Come on, Mr Bingham. They'd shoot him – or worse – for telling tales in the first place. Pass me your notebook and I'll jot – no, on second thoughts, you write down the name of the safe house."

"You won't be coming then? I thought you might introduce us."

The youth smiled: he enjoyed a joke, especially one on the edge of silliness. When he'd gone, Bingham turned to his friend with a raw laugh.

"Have we struck lucky, Brockie? You passed Senora Lamora's tip on to the Lieutenant who is now arranging to intercept this cargo. While he's holding up the shipping, we should find time to have a chat with our Serbian friends who will be waiting for the cargo to arrive. There'll be panic in the air, but everyone should be in their allotted places."

"It's a bit early to be counting our chickens, George."

"You don't have a whiff of the slight scent of success?"

"Why should these men tell us anything?"

"In exchange for avoiding a long prison sentence and being handed a ticket home?"

"They'll be armed."

"Yes, that's one fly in the ointment."

"I think I might have another talk with Lieutenant Palos. Oh, by the way, he's persuaded Senor Abad's friend – the one you shoved in the water and who nearly broke his neck on that hawser – not to press charges of assault. In return, he's let el Jefe and his friends loose, there being no hard evidence that they were involved in the assault on you."

"That's nice of him."

His friend left Bingham pondering their plight. He was nervous, experiencing true fear for perhaps the first time in his life. He hadn't expected to accost two gangsters awaiting a shipment of drugs. Bingham would have preferred to meet them quietly, perhaps annoy them a little but certainly not offer a challenge. He wondered what Brockie had in mind but supposed he knew his job: after all, once a copper always a copper.

Chapter Nine

NIGHT ON THE BEACH

Bingham waited, as Brockie, seeing the pain his friend was hiding, had suggested. It gave him time to think and he became uneasy as Brockie's intentions gradually occurred to him. His friend was going to hand Josif Bolich and Lazar Mudry over to the police. As an ex-copper he would, wouldn't he? It was the wisest thing to do, of course. Bingham could see the sense of what his friend planned. It's just that he'd have liked a chance to talk with the men himself.

"The Guardia will question them with the aid of an interpreter, George. If there's any information to be gained regarding the Mayhews, they will root it out."

"I can see that, Brockie. Nevertheless, I'd like to be there."

"At the interrogation?"

"No, at the beach. We can hire a car, arrive early and watch what goes on."

"With what purpose in mind?"

"I'm not sure. Just put my concern down to intuition. After all, it was you and I who obtained this information – not the Guardia. I think we have a right to be there at the kill."

"That could prove to be an unfortunate turn of phrase, George. All right, but we get there early and stay out of sight. Under no circumstances do we approach the house," replied Brockie, adding "You don't, by any chance, speak Serbian do you?" as though suspicious of his friend's motives.

"Grammatically."

"Grammatically?"

"It's possible to learn a language by teaching yourself the grammar and then acquiring the vocabulary. The problem is that you're somewhat stilted in its use as you lack the colloquialisms and so on. I travelled widely around Europe after I graduated and so I can get by in several countries, but I lack fluency. My Italian and Spanish are a bit like that compared, say, with Lina's. Her Italian, especially, is like a native's."

"George, you're not thinking of ..."

"No, no, of course not," replied Bingham, more or less truthfully.

But he was troubled. Bingham did not see why any of this gang should say anything to the authorities that might, however vaguely, incriminate them. If they had been involved in the Mayhews' disappearance, why should they say so? The only chance of useful information lay in the promise of a leaner sentence if they were not involved but could offer something that would lead the investigation further.

Unless they could be browbeaten in some way! Unless there was something they wanted to protect, keep hidden from the public gaze. Even then, it would have to be something more important to them than their own safety, their loyalty to the gang, their fear of Ralko Devich. Would this be information they would confide to the authorities, to the Guardia Civil, to Lieutenant Palos in person? Bingham thought not, and yet how was he to approach these men?

There was something – something someone had mentioned. Who? Who had given them anything over the past three days that might be of the slightest use? Jorge Demara, the nervous journalist? But what was it he'd said?

Bingham's pain was now cutting in badly, and his concentration was fading. Imelda Jackson brought him another beer. He smiled and thanked her, yet knowing it was the last thing he needed or wanted. What had he eaten for lunch? He couldn't remember. Leaving his beer on the table, Bingham struggled to his feet and tottered away, leaning heavily on his stick.

He knew he wasn't well. It was difficult to place one thought after another – at least one consecutive thought that linked with another. About a hundred yards from the café he reached a corner; one way led to the waterfront, the other upwards into the hills. Bingham was unsure where he was going or why. A few people passed him by on their way to siesta. One or two looked at the old man, perhaps wondering if he was in his right mind. Bingham leaned against the sun-baked wall wishing Brockie would return and help him back to the La Fonda. He needed to sleep.

A tap on the shoulder roused him. Turning with difficulty he found he was staring into the grizzled face of Fred Jackson.

"Mr Bingham, Imelda was worried. She said you didn't seem well. Come back to the café and wait for your friend."

Bingham found himself sitting at the table where he'd eaten his lunch. The surface had been cleared and wiped, the beer was gone and in its place was a cup of steaming, black coffee.

"Drink this, Senor Bingham. It will bring you round," said Imelda Jackson.

"Thank you."

"Fred will come and sit with you in a moment until your friend returns. He's a good man now, you know, Senor Bingham. Fred helps those he can."

Bingham looked up at her and smiled, wondering what was on her mind.

"He talks to the small dealers and the addicts. He tries to help."

She might work her husband to death between the marriage bed and the market, thought Bingham, but her heart was in the right place.

When Fred Jackson joined him, the man began speaking almost at once as though he wanted to give Bingham reassurance.

"We're not against bringing these people to justice, Mr Bingham. You understand that, don't you? It's just that we're afraid."

"Were you really just keeping an eye on their villa the day we arrived?"

"I had been. I knew them. As I said, I went out with Colin in his boat."

"Who sent you?"

"It was the taxi driver."

"We thought so. Was he involved?"

"No one knows for sure who was involved."

"But you have your suspicions? Everyone but my friend and I seem to know something, Mr Jackson, but no one is saying anything."

Fred Jackson was silent although it was clear he wanted to speak. Had his wife suggested he might offer Bingham some help? If so, what was it?

"What is it you want to say, Mr Jackson? How well do you know the streets?"

"Imelda told you, did she? I know all the places where drugs are sold openly. It's extremely dangerous here. The recession has forced down prices. There simply isn't the money around. The dealers are becoming desperate. It's a matter of survival for them."

"What's your interest in this, Mr Jackson?"

"I'd like to see you and your friend leave here alive – not in a wooden box. That's my interest, Mr Bingham."

His voice had suddenly become animated, even angry at Bingham's quiet persistence. To locals like Fred Jackson, Bingham could see that he was nothing but a fool. Wisdom lay not in fighting crime but in letting crime burn itself out, as Jorge Demara had suggested.

"I know that your friend is hiring a car. I can guess what for. We know the signs. Do not get involved, Mr Bingham. Stay away. Enough is enough."

It wasn't what Fred Jackson said that gave Bingham his idea; it was, rather, Imelda's comments and the man's obviously sincere wish to spare Bingham any further harm. Watching the ex-pat's face, Bingham saw not Fred Jackson but Patrick Syms and a young woman's body lying in a grubby little flat, her arm like a pincushion and needles on the floor.

"Thank you, Mr Jackson. I appreciate your concern."

Fred Jackson talked on for a while, but Bingham wasn't really listening. He'd already decided on his course of action and was now formulating a plan. It was strange how even conversations that seemed not of the slightest use at the time became the ones that turned the tide of events.

Soon after, Brockie arrived to let him know that the car had been hired and to help Bingham back to the La Fonda where he could, at last, have a desperately needed sleep. Before he dozed off, however, he arranged for Brockie to wake him in time for their trip to the beach and made two phone calls – one to Fiorenza and the other to Jorge Demara; researchers and journalists had their uses.

The package was waiting for him at the reception when Bingham went down to the hotel foyer. Whatever was in the parcel was enclosed in a tin and he thought at first that Lina had sent him a honey cake; when he unwrapped the package and opened the tin, however, Bingham found a gun. It was an automatic weapon. He knew that only from films he'd seen. He closed the tin and walked over to the bar.

"Who left this?"

"We don't know, sir. It was found on the reception desk. Your friend said not to wake you, but to wait until you came down."

"Yes, of course. Thank you."

They were seated in the hire car before Bingham showed Brockie the weapon.

"Someone's concerned for your safety, George. Have you ever used one?"

"The only weapon I'm familiar with is a 410 shotgun. My grandfather taught me to shoot when I was a child. I'm ashamed to say we shot rabbits in those days. It was a hangover from the war when they were 'off ration' and meat was scarce. Are you familiar with the weapon?"

"It's a Smith and Wesson 45 double-action semi-automatic pistol," replied Brockie, laughing at the startled expression on his friend's face. "We had a few lectures on guns so that officers would recognise one when they saw it. I must admit I went down to the firing range on a few occasions – out of interest really or perhaps it was the macho side of me coming out – but I was never licensed to use one, although I suppose I could if the need arose. Lieutenant Palos told me that they are readily available to the gangs; they take a week to deliver and cost a thousand euros a piece. Who do you think left it for you?"

"Two people come to mind, but we'll leave that for the moment. Let's go, Simon. We'll stick that thing in the glove compartment, shall we?"

"If you say so. It's loaded, by the way, but I think the binoculars I borrowed from the hotel might be of more use. They're on the back seat."

The area was not deserted as Bingham had expected. In fact, there were several houses set back from the low cliff edge. All were screened by a variety of shrubs and trees, which seemed to have self-planted themselves across the slope that ran down to the shore. There were the usual acacias, but he also recognised, much to his surprise, magnolias, viburnums, tamarisks, some trees that reminded him of laurels and the one called 'red robin' at home.

All provided good cover for the two friends, and they were grateful as they made their way from the cliff top, where Brockie had parked the car under the cover of a large magnolia, down to the beach. Bingham moved slowly and with great difficulty. Had it not been for Brockie he would never have made it.

The beach was deserted but the footprints and sandcastles, now washed down by the sea, indicated that families played there during the day. The beach was sandy. It was reddish rather than yellow sand, which Bingham found unpleasant, perhaps because it reminded him of fire. The sand was also coarse: the kind that cut tender feet.

The night was calm, and the sea surged quite gently onto the shore; it was also clear, and Bingham saw, quite easily with the aid of the binoculars Brockie had borrowed, several fishing boats bobbing offshore. He supposed one of them to be el Jefe's.

Further along the stretch of beach to their left a jetty ran out several hundred yards into the sea. Together with the natural curve of the coastline at the other end of the little bay, this formed a small harbour, which was sheltered from the view of any craft that was not positioned off the coast immediately opposite.

There was no obvious activity: the houses behind them seemed empty and the fishing boats were simply plying their legitimate trade, netting in fish that would appear on the market stalls along the Costa the following morning. The beach bars, no doubt continually active during the day, were shut for the night, a fact Bingham thought to be strange.

On the way, Brockie had told him that this stretch of the Mediterranean off the Costa del Sol was a "hotbed of crime". It was policed not only by the Spanish but also by the Royal Navy, and anyone found smuggling in the "Gateway of Hash" between Morocco and Spain would serve a long sentence in the Alhaurin prison in Malaga.

"Tension will be high tonight, George. We'd best keep quiet."

It seemed that the smugglers varied their method of operation. Sometimes, high-speed boats, similar in look to dinghies but equipped with powerful engines and known as RHIBs (rigid-hulled inflatable boats), would attempt to outrun the police and naval patrols and, if successful, land on the beaches themselves to unload their cargoes; at other times, the drugs would be dropped off on a fishing boat, which would then moor alongside a jetty such as the one they were watching.

Bingham could sense the excitement in Brockie, despite the danger in which they'd placed themselves. The thought that they might bring a "barrel-full of lowlife to justice" had whetted the ex-policeman's natural appetite for lawfulness. Bingham also noticed that his friend had brought the gun with him and was fingering it in the encroaching darkness.

They had arrived early, and time dragged. Bingham's wounds grew tighter with every hour that passed. It helped him to move but there was little opportunity for that unless he wanted to risk attracting attention to their hiding place. Brockie smiled encouragement until they could no longer see each other's faces except by the light of a very pale moon.

They heard the sound before they saw the boat. The knots in Bingham's stomach tightened. It wasn't unusual, of course, and there was no reason why a high-speed powerboat shouldn't be making its way quite legitimately along that stretch of coast but, somehow, they both knew that this was the moment for which they'd waited.

Almost immediately, and before the power boat appeared, two men were seen making their way along the wooden jetty. They walked steadily but apparently in no great hurry, going as far out from the beach as the jetty reached. The water here was at its deepest and Bingham's heart skipped the proverbial beat as he realised this would be the mooring for a boat containing the drugs. It was reasonable to suppose it would be el Jefe's fishing boat. When they reached their destination the two men stood quite calmly. Bingham could see the red spark of a cigarette in both their mouths.

Although he'd been watching as he thought carefully, Bingham did not really notice the fishing boat until the cruiser came into sight, tossing aside the white-crested waves, and pulling up alongside the smaller boat. He could see that the powerful cruiser was an impressive vessel, expensively rigged out and spotlessly clean. He could not see what passed between the boats, but the deed was done speedily. Within minutes, the cruiser powered off, turning sharply back the way it had come, leaving the fishing boat swaying fretfully in its wake.

Nothing happened for what seemed to be a long time, but eventually the fishing boat turned and headed gracefully towards the jetty and the waiting men. It moored neatly, rocking only slightly in the swell. The wheelhouse was between Bingham and the two men on the jetty and so it was difficult for him to see exactly what was happening until the fishermen left their vessel and formed a human chain, passing crates from one to another until a pile was stacked neatly partway to the beach.

Bingham looked inland, wondering where the 'safe house' might be, and saw the roof of a dwelling hidden by a copse of magnolia trees. There were no lights shining from the house as far as he could see and the men were working without torches or lamps, relying entirely on the moon.

Soon the human chain moved beyond the pile of crates and began passing them further along the jetty. Bingham supposed that once the crates were stored in the house the fishermen would return to their boat leaving only the two Serbs with the hash. This would make it easier for what he had in mind, which was to approach the men on his own, leaving Brockie with the hire car in case things went wrong.

He knew the risks involved but had faith in his powers of persuasion – those and the name of Ralko Devich with whom he had struck up an acquaintance: at least that was the impression he was hoping to convey.

It was as these slightly hopeful thoughts were passing through his mind and he was about to favour Brockie with a smile that the two Guardia Civil officers appeared on the beach. They had come from the direction in which the crates were headed, and Bingham supposed they had already examined the house. They swept the beach with their spotlights and picked out the men on the jetty and el Jefe's boat at its mooring.

The men froze and lowered the crates. A sharp command came from the fishing boat and Bingham recognised el Jefe's voice. Bingham also noticed Brockie remove the automatic pistol from his pocket and fiddle with what he supposed to be the safety catch. The policemen stood quite still, holding their spotlights steady on the smugglers. There was a brief smattering of voices, all subdued, and one of the men walked across the beach towards the officers.

Bingham was too far away to hear what was said but he saw through his binoculars that money passed hands. The policemen then walked with the smuggler to the jetty and joined the chain that was passing the hash up the beach to the house where it would be stored until it was "repackaged in smaller containers and make its way through Spain and then France to Amsterdam unless it's going to be distributed locally through someone like me". Bingham heard Richard Brown's words as clearly as when the young man had spoken them.

He looked at Brockie, whose face was crestfallen and who was making the weapon safe before replacing it in his pocket. It had been in his mind to help if the Guardia officers were in trouble. Now it was apparent they were in league with the smugglers, only he and Bingham faced any danger.

"I'm sorry, Simon. I was beginning to think, like you, that Lieutenant Palos was an honest man. It would appear he's managed this operation very smoothly. Whoever delivered the drugs has cruised off, el Jefe and his men will return to Guaro (probably with a catch for the local market) and his officers may even lend a hand repackaging the hash."

"It would appear so, George, it would appear so."

The two friends waited until the unloading of the contraband was complete and the wooden crates had finally vanished from the beach. It didn't take long, and soon the fishermen were returning to their boat, sharing a laugh and a smoke, looking forward to resuming their traditional role, their pockets soon to be swelling with the pay-out from the drugs.

"Shall we go home, George?"

Bingham wasn't sure whether his friend meant Northfield, England or the La Fonda, Guaro del Mar. Either way, Bingham had other ideas.

"I have just one more hand to play, Simon. But first, yes, the La Fonda for a shower and a change of bandages and clothes. We might have a long day ahead of us. Might I borrow the gun?"

Chapter Ten
TRIP TO THE HILLS

It was, in fact, nearer coffee time before Bingham could make a move: the email he was expecting from Fiorenza and the memoranda he was expecting from Jorge Demara did not arrive until mid-morning. The delay enabled him to snatch a rather long catnap and so by the time he and Brockie were sitting in the hotel foyer enjoying a black coffee and a cappuccino Bingham was feeling refreshed. He outlined to Brockie what he had in mind.

"I understand from Senor Demara that Ralko Devich can be found in his offices above the casino he owns at this time of the day, Simon. I want you to drive us there – it's on the Calle Huerta Nueva – and stay in the car. Put this gun in the glove compartment. Do not interfere with the gun in any way and leave the compartment unlocked."

"I don't like this scheme of yours, George."

"Nor do I, but Ralko Devich is a family man, and I think he'll understand my concern."

Would he? Much depended on Bingham's ability to create an impression, such as an actor does on stage. He had performed many times in Norwich theatres, and this situation required that he put on an act. But what act, and how?

"If I'm successful," he continued, "I will be accompanied by one of his men. I imagine he might be armed. I'll leave that side of things to you."

"Thanks, George. And if this Devich doesn't cooperate?"

"Be positive, Simon. My glass is half full."

"Mine has only a few dregs in the bottom."

They were both nervous. Bingham recalled his interview for university when, despite his good A level grades, so much seemed to hang on the impression he might make. It seemed a long time ago: it was over fifty years. He laughed quietly to himself. How could anyone in their right mind compare facing a panel of dons to facing one of the nastiest gangsters on the Costa del Sol? Somehow, this moment threw his whole life and all its little worries into perspective. Or did it? Next spring he'd still be worrying about how many of his bees had survived the winter.

The casino was situated on a tree-lined side street of the town. It was quiet and cool in the morning heat, which was now building to midday temperatures of thirty plus. If he was successful, they were in for a long, hot drive but at least the car was air-conditioned.

Again, he smiled at his concern for the relatively trivial things of life. How many times during the years he and Lina were raising their children – Paul, who was a doctor and the only one married; Cecilia and Fiorenza, the twins, one a politician's secretary, the other a researcher for the BBC; Ben, the chemist, his youngest and the one to whom he was closest – had they driven through the countries of Europe without air-conditioning but with the windows open? He knew why he was thinking of his children and his beloved wife at that moment, of course, and it only increased his nervousness.

A nervousness enhanced by the sight of the man who blocked his path as he approached the casino. There was no humour in any aspect of the man's face – not in his lips, his lines or his eyes. Bingham decided that his mouth had never broken into a smile. He was as big as the proverbial shithouse – Bingham recalled that phrase from some gangster novel he'd read in his teens – and looked as though one of his greatest pleasures might be in hitting someone as hard as possible.

"Move the car."

"I've come hoping to see Senor Devich."

"He sees no one. Move the car."

His first sentence had been spoken in Spanish; the second, in English.

"Are you from Serbia?"

The man looked blankly at Bingham, weighing him up, concerned with the possibility of a threat, eyeing Brockie in the parked car, perhaps wondering if he was dealing with a nincompoop.

"I've always been impressed with the grasp of languages that so many Europeans possess," continued Bingham, "You put us English to shame."

"Move the car. Mr Devich sees no one," said the man, clenching his fist.

"It's a family matter. It concerns Velimer. I'm sure Senor Devich will see me."

"Wait."

Bingham turned and smiled at Brockie as the man walked into the casino. A few moments later they saw a curtain move on the first floor and a window was pushed slightly open. Bingham looked up and smiled, but the figures were invisible to him. All he saw was the morning sun reflected on the window.

When the man reappeared, he was as sullen as ever.

"He will see you. Take the car to the back and wait. You come with me."

Both Brockie and Bingham obeyed.

Once he was inside, the man shoved Bingham against a wall and ran his hands over him. Searching for weapons, Bingham thought, until his wallet and passport were removed, and he realised they were after identification as well.

Despite his trepidation at being where he was, Bingham couldn't help noticing the interior of the casino and being disappointed. The habits of a lifetime are, perhaps, hard to kick even in extreme circumstances. The casino was housed in an old building. From the street, a passer-by would have taken it as being a rather grand, three-storey house; but the inside had been gutted and 'refurbished' – Bingham hung on to that word in his mind – in the style of any casino from Great Yarmouth to Las Vegas. It lacked the style of the traditional French casinos; its owners had chosen what was considered chic: plastic, glass, metal, bright colours and flashy lighting.

The contrast between the exterior and interior of the building made Bingham think again about Guaro. It was two worlds really, he thought, with one hiding the other; there was no connection, let alone harmony, between where he found himself and the cafes of the waterfront. He was in an alien environment.

The staircase was narrow and decorated with studio shots of old Hollywood stars: Sinatra, Garbo, Monroe, Gable, Martin – name them and they were there. What had these people to do with the Spaniards he'd met, friendly or otherwise, Bingham thought. His answer was 'nothing'.

The first landing opened out onto a series of rooms and the muscle man led him to one overlooking the main street. Behind a desk he obviously considered imposing was a man who could only have been Ralko Devich; no introduction was necessary, and none was given. The door shut behind Bingham and he faced the man he'd come to see; he was about to play his last card.

Courtesy wasn't in the man's manner; he neither stood, as might have been expected in any civilised society, nor greeted Bingham. He merely sat watching him through eyes so narrow that Bingham could not detect the colour.

Bingham was never one to beat about the bush and saw no reason to change the habits of a lifetime. He placed the photograph of Colin and Patty Mayhew, which he had taken from their villa, on the desk.

Ralko Devich's eyes never flickered as he gazed at the couple before looking up at Bingham and fixing him with a long stare. Bingham saw the colour as he returned the stare. The man's eyes were a dark brown and the colour was accentuated by the widened pupil in the dark room. He never spoke but continued to watch Bingham.

"My I sit down? I've had rather a bad accident and standing for long is painful."

There was no answer, and so Bingham took a chair from its place near the far wall and eased himself onto it.

The far wall was covered with photographs that could only have been the gangster's family. Prominent was a young woman, quite beautiful with long, dark hair and laughing eyes. In one photograph she was with a man who matched her in looks, and who was obviously Ralko Devich when he was younger. It was a wedding photograph, taken in a village street; the couple were surrounded by family and friends who were showering them with flowers and petals. In another, the same woman was surrounded by four children; they were in a park somewhere, and there was a roundabout and a witch's hat behind them. A third showed some sort of family celebration; two of the children were watching another being baptised in its mother's arms. In a fourth, the woman, now older, was sitting on a sofa with the children posed around her.

"You are clearly a family man, Senor Devich," said Bingham, indicating the photographs, "and it is to your understanding I wish to appeal. My friend and I have no official status in Guaro. We have come on behalf of Colin and Patty's family. The family want to know where they are. If they are missing, they would like them found. If they are dead, they would like them returned for a Christian burial. I have no interest in your work here. That is the concern of others."

He paused, hoping for some response: perhaps a twitch of the mouth, a hint of comprehension in the eyes. There was nothing. It was as though the man was dead to any kind of human thoughts outside the immediate concern for his own survival. Bingham knew from Fiorenza's memoranda that in Serbia as a young man Ralko Devich had gained the acceptance of his kind by stabbing to death a policeman; it had been his initiation into the gang. He'd never looked back but continued to mete out torture and death with knife, gun, fist and foot or whatever came to hand to anyone who crossed his path.

"It has not actually been suggested to me that they worked for you, but merely that you might know where they have gone."

Bingham felt foolish attempting to assuage any misgivings the man might have for he clearly possessed none; but it is difficult holding a conversation with someone who remains silent, and Bingham needed a response of some kind. Was sitting quietly, waiting for a response, his only option? It had worked during his career.

Sitting watching the gangster, Bingham wondered whether there was any intelligence or feeling in the man at all or whether his normal emotional faculties had simply been honed down to the essential, rather like those of animals. Perhaps after a lifetime of dishing out terror, Ralko Devich was equipped only to stay alive, to kill, feed and pass on. Bingham thought of creatures such as wolves or lions and how they clearly possessed a real sense of family, caring for their young, playing together; but he wouldn't have chosen to be in their company when they were hungry or fearful.

When the silence dragged on, Bingham, concerned that he might be thrown onto the street with no further lead as to where the Mayhews might be, turned and indicated the photographs.

"This is your family? They live in England, I believe."

It was the only card he had left, and a dangerous one to play. When the man spoke, his voice was little more than a rasp. Bingham was reminded of the sound he heard as a boy, watching his father working on the lathe he kept in the garden shed, shaping a piece of wood with chisel and file. His father had been a solicitor – a job with its natural anxieties, and the lathe had always soothed him.

"You came to speak of Velimer, my son."

"I simply used his name to gain a few words with you. I have never met your son."

"You knew his name."

Bingham placed the list of names and addresses he had garnered from Fiorenza and Jorge Demara onto the desk. They were members of Ralko Devich's family or friends – all except one who Bingham had yet to place.

"Where did you get these names?"

"I asked a journalist in Great Britain. No one here would talk about you, but you are known to the British authorities and I needed to speak with you. You are the only man who may be able to help me."

"You said you were not a policeman."

"I'm not. I was a schoolteacher and I have taught many children. One of them is a journalist. Newspapers hold much information that they do not print."

Bingham hoped that Ralko Devich would get his drift, since spelling it out precisely would threaten both the man and his family. Bingham assessed that an apprehensive Devich was not the kind of animal he would wish to face.

The gangster lifted his eyes from the paper and looked at Bingham. They showed instinct rather than thought. Should he kill or move on – nothing more. Devich looked like an old wolf, the alpha male, his face scarred by the need to remain dominant. How many challenges had he fought off? How many had he left cut and bleeding to remain leader of the pack? There was no doubt in Bingham's mind that the animal he faced was violent, one who could not bear to be crossed, one who would not, could not, leave an enemy alive.

Had Bingham been a young man, had he been a local, the impression he was giving would have been more intimidating, occasioning an immediate attack. But he wasn't: he was just an old man, wounded and slumped in a chair.

"Who beat you?"

"I'm not sure, but I think it was a group of men I'd met on the waterfront."

"Why?"

He mustn't give too much information: just enough to keep this wolf at bay.

"I'd been asking about the Mayhews. They didn't seem to like my questions. It was dark. They attacked me in the street. I didn't see them. It was … late in the day."

"Who knows you have come to ask for my help?"

"Apart from my friend there is no one in Guaro."

"Who gave you my name?"

The rasping voice was so flat, almost as though the speaker had no interest in the answers other than to ascertain who was to be taught a final lesson. Devich couldn't allow anyone to think he was soft. His enemies had to be punished: only fear of him would stop their defiance.

"You are known to the Guardia as a respectable businessman. It was the only name I had that might have been of any use. I needed a man of influence in the community. I knew a respectable businessman would help me if he could."

His answer confused even Bingham. He simply hoped it was vague enough to suggest that the gangster's name had emerged in conversation, unconnected with any suggestion of criminal activities. Confusion was all he had to offer, and death was all he could expect; a name was out of the question.

"He was my friend. I want to find him."

It was instinct made Bingham say what he did: instinct and his experience as an actor. How many times on stage were the audience encouraged to listen between the lines?

How many times in rehearsal had a good director insisted that words, however apparently insignificant, should not been thrown away.

He was desperate now to create the impression of an old fool seeking old friends to bring them home to rest; an old fool, not knowing quite what he was doing, grasping at names like straws in the wind.

Another long silence followed. Ralko Devich watched him as the hunter watches its prey, waiting for that moment of weakness, waiting for the hunted to run, to give any sign that it had accepted defeat, accepted the right of the hunter to kill.

Eventually he pulled a note pad towards him, wrote a few words on the sheet of paper and handed it to Bingham.

"Give my man this note," he said, "and he will see to you."

Bingham took the sheet and waited while Devich lifted the phone and made a call, speaking in English as he had done throughout their interview. While he was on the phone, Bingham glanced down at the message on the pad. It was written in Serbian. When he looked up, he saw for the first time a smile on the gangster's face. It was only a pull of the mouth, but it was a smile.

A few moments later, a third gangster walked into the room. Bingham wondered whether he was one of the two they had seen on the beach the previous night.

"Mr Bingham wants to take a trip to the hills, Dobrilo. I have made a note of his requirements. He has them in his hand. You are to carry them out as I have said … No harm will come to you. Mr Bingham just wants to be reunited with his friends."

He turned to Bingham.

"My friend, Dobrilo Petrof will look after you, Mr Bingham."

Ralko Devich said no more. He leaned back in his chair and watched the two men leave his office. He reached out for a cigar from the box marked 'Havana' on his desk. It was an ostentatious move, as pretentious as the cigar box, and Bingham was not surprised. Devich was in command; he controlled the destinies of those who might be foolish enough to cross him. Bingham had been stalked by an experienced carnivore and the animal had every reason to be pleased.

Dobrilo Petrof took the note from Bingham, smiled and gestured to the doorman who walked to the back of the casino along a side passage and emerged a few minutes later with a parcel of sacking. It was a long parcel and one that was heavy. Bingham could only guess what it might contain as he watched the gangster place it carefully in the boot of the car

Once in the hire car, Bingham indicated to Dobrilo Petrof that he should sit next to Brockie, who was to drive. He then placed the photograph and lists in the glove compartment before making himself comfortable in the back seat.

It was a relatively short drive, no more than half-an-hour, through the increasingly dry terrain of the Andalusian hills. This must have been the way the Mayhews came, thought Bingham, knowing his first instincts had been true. All fear had left him, dwindling away as the car made its difficult ascent along the narrow road, dwindling away as he imagined the fear in the hearts of the old couple, knowing as they must have done that this was to be their final journey. How much, he wondered, had Patty Mayhew known of her husband's plight. Thinking about Patty, Bingham felt his fear replaced by anger.

Once clear of Guaro, the road followed a narrow river valley, making its way steadily towards the ridge. They passed nothing on the way except a goatherd tending his animals, and finally pulled the car to a halt beside a small copse. Across the valley, Bingham saw small villages, their white walls reflected in the afternoon sun.

Dobrilo Petrof moved casually from the car and strolled towards the boot. There was arrogance in his manner. He was a man who felt in control of the situation. He reached for the boot catch as Brockie moved in behind him, spread his legs and slipped the gun from the gangster's holster. The gangster's surprise was only matched by Bingham's, who had never seen his friend's professional skills active before.

"I think your words were 'I'll leave that side of things to you', George," said Brockie with a smile.

The gangster's surprise had been quickly replaced by a nonchalance bordering on indifference. He eyed both men with a mixture of amusement and contempt. Brockie's action, apparently so decisive a few moments before, seemed to make no impression on the Serb.

"Senor Petrof, I think you'd better carry on. Your boss's note made everything clear, didn't it? The slight difference, I believe, is that we were to dig our own graves – if my knowledge of Serbian is not too far off the mark. George, stand clear. Senor Petrof has a pick and shovel in the boot. I'd hate him to catch you round the head with it. We were to be shot and buried alongside Colin and Patty Mayhew whose lives ended on this spot."

A frown crossed the gangster's face, but only for a second. He and his boss may have been outsmarted and outgunned, but he clearly felt in control.

"You English are soft, old-fashioned. You do not like to hurt people. Your friend will not shoot. There is the spot," said Dobrilo Petrof, nodding to a pile of rocks beside the road. "Dig up your friends for yourselves."

Brockie indicated that the gangster was to stand aside, which he did, and then the ex-policeman removed the tools from the boot and removed the sacking, after passing Bingham the gun with an order to keep the gangster "covered".

"I'll do the digging, George. You're not in a fit state."

The earth, although baked dry by the Spanish sun, crumbled easily from the shovel once Brockie had removed the top layer of soil. Occasionally the ex-policeman looked across at the gangster, as if for reassurance that this was the right spot. He placed the shovel carefully each time, conscious that he was digging towards two corpses that had been buried there for some time, conscious that their burial would have lacked any kind of ceremony, any kind of care including the use, even, of a blanket.

The gangster continued to lean against the side of the car, smoking cigarette after cigarette, gazing across the valley, ignoring the two men he obviously still considered his captives.

"Is it always this way when a cargo is lost?" asked Bingham, speaking deliberately in Serbian, hoping to ease the man into sharing a confidence.

Dobrilo Petrof looked at him, perhaps wondering just how much Bingham understood, how much had passed between him and his boss, Ralko Devich.

"If they lose it, they must pay. That is the rule."

"But if it was an accident?"

Dobrilo Petrof shrugged.

"The law is the law. There is no other way. Payment is made or payment is taken. It's the carrier's job to look after the goods."

"Were you the one who took the payment?"

The phrase seemed to amuse the Serb.

"There have been worse ways of making the payment," he said, "One who couldn't pay is working off his debt in a gay brothel. I know what I would prefer," he said with a laugh.

"I've dug far enough," said Brockie, "We need professional help now, George."

The gangster walked over to the grave and looked in as though admiring his efforts at gardening.

"They died in each other's arms," he said, sauntering back to the car.

It was the moment for which Bingham had been waiting. He threw Brockie a quick glance as Dobrilo Petrof opened the glove compartment, took out the gun and levelled it at Bingham, who sat slumped on the outcrop of rocks.

"Now it is your turn to join your friends."

The gangster pulled the trigger. Brockie started forward as the dull click was heard. Before Dobrilo Petrof had time to realise what had happened, Brockie struck him across the back with the shovel and the gangster sprawled gasping for breath in the Spanish dust. By the time he was fully aware of the trick played on him, Dobrilo Petrof's hands were tied with Brockie's tie and the ex-policeman was securing the killer's feet with his own belt.

"You could have told me what you were up to, George."

"You knew."

"Only because I realised you'd removed the cartridges from the gun when I put it in the glove compartment."

"A nod is as good as a wink to a man like you, Simon. Knowing the gun was there put our friend at his ease, and that's what I wanted."

Bingham gave Dobrilo Petrof a quick smile, which the gangster failed to return.

"When were you certain of what had happened to the Mayhews?"

"Certain would be too strong a word, Simon, but it was something Camila Julio said that made me realise what we'd both thought from the beginning was probably the truth."

"I think I'll give our Lieutenant Palos a bell, George. It's time he came around to our way of thinking."

Chapter Eleven

OUR MAN AT HOME

The lieutenant was all smiles when he arrived on the scene and during their ride back to Guaro; and Brockie, too, had what Bingham considered an unwarranted smugness about him. He had, of course, only muttered "it would appear so" as they'd left the beach, believing the Guardia officer to have been in league with the drug smugglers; and Brockie had, at the beginning, affirmed his conviction that Lieutenant Palos was a good copper. 'I can assure you that Palos is straight': Bingham could hear his friend's words and see it in his smile.

It transpired that the two officers on the beach had subsequently arrested Bolich and Mudry, el Jefe and his men had been picked up on their return to Guaro and the cruiser that had carried the drugs from Morocco had been waylaid on its attempted return.

"Their faces were a picture," said Lieutenant Palos.

"Rather like yours at the moment, George," said Brockie with a smile at his friend.

"I must thank you gentlemen for the information you passed on. It is a fine example of the spirit of cooperation between our two countries."

"Is the mayor, Senor Garcas, pleased?" asked Bingham.

The lieutenant smiled.

"You see corruption everywhere, Senor Bingham."

"Not at all! I simply have the impression that your people tend to turn a blind eye as long as it doesn't involve one of your own citizens."

"We questioned Bolich and Mudry all morning, but they said nothing. The gang is their life, you see. The only way out of the gang is in a coffin. However, Eusebio and his friends were persuaded to talk as long as they were convinced that we could put the whole gang behind bars."

"You offered them a lighter sentence?" asked Brockie.

Lieutenant Palos shrugged.

"We arrested Senor Devich after he'd finished his lunch. By tonight you will find Eusebio and his friends back on the waterfront."

Strangely, Bingham found himself not really minding the compromise. Guaro once had a life of its own before the scum arrived, first from Britain and, more recently, from Eastern Europe. The people of the Costa del Sol hadn't invited these gangsters to make their home there, and Bingham felt sorry for the Spaniards involved.

"It will not be too difficult, presumably, to lay the killing of Colin and Patty Mayhew at their door?"

"It will take some legal diplomacy, but we will have your evidence to rely on, Senor Bingham."

"You knew that Colin, at least, was involved with Devich's gang?"

"We suspected some connection but there was no evidence. We could trace no large sums of money to Senor Mayhew's account. He was not a man who had any obvious links to drug smuggling."

"No," replied Bingham, "And that still remains the case."

"Tell me, Senor Bingham, how you managed to persuade Senor Devich to take you to the grave."

"I placed a list on his desk. It contained the names of his family. Ralko Devich had dropped them off in Britain on his way to the Costa del Sol so that the British taxpayer could look after them while he was away. Senor Devich believed I had obtained the list from a journalist friend and didn't like to think that information might appear in the newspapers."

The lieutenant laughed.

Both friends were glad that they were not involved in the gathering and collating of the evidence that might convict Devich and his men – Brockie, as an ex-policeman and with many memories of the long hours involved. It was with distinct relief that they left the Guardia lieutenant to his task – a task that would, eventually, involve making the arrangements for what remained of the bodies of Colin and Patty Mayhew to be flown home for a decent burial.

"Where to now, George?" asked Brockie as they said farewell to the Lieutenant Palos.

"Take your choice, Simon. You can either come with me to return our gun to its owner or contact your colleagues in the National Criminal Intelligence Service. There was one name on the list that didn't belong to Devich's family and I think the man might be worth tracing."

"I'll contact my ex-colleagues later in the day, George. I could do with a drink and we missed lunch."

Imelda Jackson was still hot and bothered when they arrived but as welcoming as ever: two ice cold beers were placed before them and Bingham's request to know her 'speciality of the day' met with pleasure.

"It will be a wait, Senor Bingham. The siesta is but lately over and …"

She raised her arms to the heavens.

"Podemos hablar con tu marido?" asked Bingham.

Imelda Jackson gave Bingham a smile that would have melted the oldest of hearts and swung off to the café where she opened a door by the bar that led to the upstairs rooms.

"Fred! Senor Bingham quiere hablar con usted."

"You're a flirt, George," said Brockie.

"Not at all. We Brits should try our best with other languages. It's polite."

Fred Jackson emerged quickly, tucking in his shirt, listened to a few words from his wife and came over to where the two friends sat with their beers.

"A drink, Fred?"

"No, I'd better not. Imelda's got a few chores for me. What can I do for you?"

Brockie placed the automatic pistol on the table.

"Thanks," he said, "It saved our lives."

Fred Jackson grabbed the weapon and stuffed it quickly into a trouser pocket.

"How did you know it was mine?"

"It could only have been you or young Brown, and you were the favourite choice," replied Brockie.

"I take it you've been busy during siesta, Fred?" asked Bingham.

"You might say that," replied Fred Jackson with a slight smile.

"So, you won't have heard the latest news? Let me bring you up to date."

The ex-drug dealer listened while Bingham outlined what had happened since coffee time that morning. The old man's face was a mosaic of emotions: relief that the Serbians were under arrest, anxiety when he heard of el Jefe's impending release and an outpouring of sorrow when Bingham spoke of the Mayhews. Tears welled in the man's eyes: tears released from a long-held suspicion.

"You found Colin and Patty?" he asked, wanting that part of the story repeated.

"Yes."

"They'd taken that 'trip to the hills'?"

"Yes. I think you can fill in the details, can't you, Fred? Linking Colin with drug dealing was the difficult part, since he appeared to have no unexpected funds. When I heard he'd helped one of the locals, with Brockie having seen no unusual amounts drawn from his accounts, I began to wonder."

"Camila and Betran?

"Yes."

"Colin was like that – he'd do anything for anyone. It was a good way of using bad money. He didn't want to be involved and was determined never to benefit from what he did. Colin had no choice. When the Serbian mob heard he made regular, legitimate trips to Malaga he became their prime target for use as what your press calls a drugs mule. He had no choice. It was either go along with what they wanted, or watch Patty being raped by a couple of them."

"Go on."

"He'd park the car, leaving it unlocked, while he collected his rents. When he came back the drugs had gone from the boot and the payment was in its place. Until one day, it wasn't. Colin didn't know what had gone wrong. It was unlikely the people he delivered to would have done him because the Serbs wouldn't have liked that. He could only guess that someone had watched and stolen the shipment. He was in one helluver state, I can tell you, and I couldn't help him. I didn't have that kind of money."

"What happened to the money he'd already made?"

"He gave it away or helped people like the Julios. Sometimes, he dumped his cut in litter bins across Malaga – just to get rid of it. Some of them down-and-outs must have thought their prayers had been answered when they searched the bins for food and fags. Other times, I suppose the stuff was just dumped by the dustmen."

"I suppose Patty knew nothing of this business?"

"No. Colin thought she'd just worry herself sick."

The three men sat quietly thinking of the old lady being driven to her death by the Serbian gangsters, not knowing why she was standing on the edge of her grave locked in her husband's arms.

"Thanks, Fred. Tell Imelda that we'll be back for our evening meal. Brockie has a call to make and I want the medics to check my cuts and bruises."

There seemed no point in asking why Fred Jackson hadn't told them what he knew on that first morning, of pointing out how much time would have been saved. In a town like Guaro del Mar fear hung around on street corners, lounged in bars, shared dinner in restaurants and stood admiring the waterfront.

Bingham, nevertheless, was sad when he and Brockie left the Spanish resort the following day, having given their statements, made their promises to return and said their goodbyes. They left a charming people bedevilled by criminals. The only consolation Bingham felt was in not having to play a round of golf with Brockie.

It was just a week later that he sat in the carpark of a shopping mall to the north of London. Brockie had done all the work through his old associates in the NCIS and everyone was now waiting for the final count. It was the name on the list – Marko Stefanich – that had attracted, first, Bingham's attention and, secondly, Brockie's searches. The name had stuck out and so had the address since neither matched any other on the list.

Bingham had quite simply written to the man asking to see him, claiming to have information that might lead to the taking of revenge on those responsible for the capture of Ralko Devich. The authorities had been reluctant to use Bingham until it became clear that he knew more of the situation at first hand than anyone else.

"Besides," he said, "My injuries lend authenticity to my purpose."

Most reluctant of all had been Brockie.

"There's no need for this, George. The man's organisation in Guaro is broken, and the NCIS boys and girls will have him sooner or later."

"Marko Stefanich is the gang's man in Britain, Simon. He's the hub of this vile organisation. I don't like the idea of him living here among decent people, and I can't get the sight of Colin and Patty Mayhew digging their own grave, while those bastards stood and watched, out of my mind."

He arrived in the car park, dropped by taxi, having spent the previous evening with Fiorenza at her London flat. The mall was crowded with shoppers and Bingham, without looking about him, strolled over to the main entrance and waited. He didn't wait for long. The man who approached him did so from behind and ran his hands over Bingham, searching for weapons, almost before Bingham realized what was happening. When he turned with difficulty, Bingham found himself facing a fat man with plump cheeks and a bald head; he was the very likeness of the bouncer at the casino and Bingham started with apprehension.

The man said nothing but indicated that Bingham should follow him. They reached a large, dark-coloured car parked under the shade of some trees at the far end of the carpark, and Bingham was shoved into the back seat. He feared briefly that he might be driven off but soon noticed the car was driverless. Beside him sat Marko Stefanich, his lean face pared almost to the bone, his eyes barely open and his mouth almost lipless.

Bingham wondered how people like this man related to others in any normal way. He remembered the same thoughts occurring when he'd seen the photographs on the wall of Ralko Devich's office. Did such men know how to love? Bingham doubted it.

Stefanich looked him over but said nothing. Bingham had rehearsed the story he was going to tell. At least, he had a story with a beginning and an end; it was the middle bits that were going to prove difficult.

"I was a schoolteacher," he said, "I am now retired, and I was on holiday in Guaro del Mar. One night as I was walking back to my hotel, the La Fonda, a young man approached offering me drugs. I don't take drugs. I don't approve of drugs. I don't like people who deal in drugs. So, I reported him to the Guardia Civil."

Neither Brockie nor the NCIS officers had approved of the way Bingham intended to open his story; but he had insisted, pointing out that above all else he must not appear to be attempting to gain Stefanich's confidence and certainly not his approval.

"The following day the police officers rounded the young man up and I identified him. They took him by surprise and so, when they searched his flat, they found enough hash and cocaine to bring about a conviction.

That should have been the end of the story. What more can you ask for than a scumbag behind bars? But his friends didn't share that point of view, and so the next night when I was walking back to my hotel from one of the waterfront restaurants, the Toro Puerto Marina, they set about me.

I don't know what would have happened if a couple of your lads – Josef and Lazar by name – hadn't chipped in and helped me. They seemed to resent what these blokes were doing. They kept talking about 'their territory' and were more than upset, I can tell you."

"No one takes over our territory," said Stefanich, angrily, "No one. We are the law where we operate in the town. A while back, a bunch of Romanians tried to use our men to smuggle hash. We shot them all dead and had their bodies dumped out at sea."

"Eusebio and his friends?"

"Yes."

"You spend time in Guaro yourself?"

"I go over occasionally to see that Ralko and the boys are behaving themselves."

"You are close," he said, laughing, encouraging Stefanich to continue.

"We come from the same village. We grew up together. Back home it is the only way to make a living."

"You remind me of a young man I spoke with in Guaro. He, too, had to earn his living in such a way. A family matter: he had a wife and children."

Disapproval wasn't something to which Stefanich was accustomed, but Bingham was aiming to antagonise the gangster. He caught the expression in the man's eyes as they widened slightly.

"A wife!" laughed Stefanich, emphasising the 'a', "I have one in each country and a mistress on the side in both places." He added, as though an afterthought, "There are things you can do with a mistress that you wouldn't do with your wife."

"The young man dealt only in hash, and in a small way. He was forever looking over his shoulder in case he was being watched."

"I have friends in high places. I have no such problems. All borders are open to me. It is a question of trust, of knowing the people you work with. As I said, we are a family."

"And the only way out is in a coffin – yes? Senor Devich told me that was the way."

"You spoke with Ralko?"

"His men took me to the medical centre. He paid the bill, and so I went to thank him. He told me – much as you have done – that territory is sacred, that even the Italian Mafia does not tread on your toes."

"The Mafia! In the north of Italy, they work for us. Even the priests are afraid."

The coldness of the man was never more apparent to Bingham than when he made that remark. What he said could have been taken as a boast. It was anything but: Marko Stefanich sounded just like any other businessman discussing his contacts, products and method of working. It was all cut and dried, carefully minded, simply an operation through which he earned a living. The torture, mutilation, rape and murder involved were just part and parcel of the way business was done.

"Senor Devich said that the coming down of borders across Europe had been of great benefit his to his work."

Marko Stefanich laughed.

"We have different identities in different places. Genuine fake passports are easy to come by. It is simply a question of money. I could arrange a new life for you in Spain, Mr Sanders."

Bingham smiled, both at Marko Stefanich's use of the name he'd assumed and the man's description of false passports as "genuine fakes". While on holiday in Turkey, he and Lina had been lured to a back-street warehouse where the trader extolled his "genuine fake" Gucci handbags as being distinct from the less genuine fakes available on the beach. Bingham relayed his story, but Stefanich wasn't interested.

"I don't think my wife would approve of me having a new life, Mr Stefanich."

The gangster looked at Bingham, contempt expressed on his face.

"No one here or in Spain knows my real name, Mr Sanders. Even in my own country I have several names and several addresses, depending on where I am travelling. If the authorities cannot trace you, what chance has a wife?"

He did laugh at his own joke. Bingham wondered whether the English sense of humour had rubbed off on him or whether wife jokes were common across the world.

"Besides, the justice system in my country is in the hands of those who can be trusted," said Stefanich, asserting, once again, the right of any businessman to function free of police interference. "What else did Ralko tell you?" he asked, suddenly.

"We talked of his family. He is very much the family man, but prefers to keep them safe in Britain rather than have them share the risks he faces on the Costa del Sol."

"We are all family men. You disapprove of drugs and those of us who deal in drugs. But we are merely businessmen. We do not ask people to take drugs. We do not invite or coerce them. Such people make their own choices. We provide what they need. It is like any other business: you find a loophole in the market and supply the product."

"What of those who work for you but are not in the family/" asked Bingham, stressing the last three words, realising his mistake as soon as he spoke. He'd led Stefanich until that moment; now, he was asking questions.

"A man can expect loyalty of his employees. Who did you have in mind?"

"Those who work for you along the waterfront," replied Bingham, quickly.

"Finish what you came to tell me. You have the name of the man who betrayed us?"

"They – the men who helped me, Josef and Lazar – were taking hold of a shipment on one of the beaches … along the coast from Guaro del Mar. The man concerned came across them … He … excuse me. Do you mind if we talk outside the car? I need to stretch my legs. The wounds still tend to seize up."

"We will talk where we are. It is private."

"Then perhaps I could just stretch my legs."

Bingham had to leave the car: it was to be the signal, but he could hardly struggle against Stefanich if the gangster decided to hold him down.

"How did you know of the shipment?"

"You will remember I mentioned the men on the waterfront to you?"

Stefanich said nothing.

"The fishermen."

The gangster, still silent, tensed.

"They were known to the young man and his friends."

"You mean the friends of the young man – the ones who beat you?"

"Excuse me," said Bingham, "the cramp – I must relieve this cramp."

The gangster watched as Bingham hobbled from the car and stretched his legs, appearing to be relieving the pain of having sat so long. He reached out with his arms. He looked round. Two men – the one who had searched him in front of the mall and another – had emerged swiftly from a Range Rover in a parking space across the carpark from where Bingham and Stefanich had talked.

The gangster swung his legs out and stood beside Bingham. He signalled to the two men. They moved as though to return to their vehicle.

Bingham wasn't sure how long he'd stood leaning on the bonnet of Marko Stefanich's car. It had to be five minutes, didn't it?

"Yes," he rambled, "It was a friend of a young man, but not that young man. He was a fiction – someone I made up as part of my tale. I suppose you could call it a tale. Others might use the term 'baloney'. I suppose it depends how you view its purpose."

He was talking rubbish. Marko Stefanich looked at him, his face puzzled and then anxious. Bingham saw the gangster trying to make a connection. So much of

Bingham's tale had been true. Stefanich would have known the details from the remnants of his mob in Guaro or through the Moroccan connection. Knowing that had been Bingham's strength. He also understood that a convincing liar kept as near the truth as possible. It was always a question of perception.

"There was another young man involved, you see. He was the one who picked me up from the pavement ..."

Marko Stefanich was uncertain. Bingham could see the man's doubts rising in anger. The gangster wasn't sure but had his suspicions. You don't live his kind of life by trusting anyone outside the family. Shoot first and ask questions later.

Bingham never knew what hit him. It was some kind of cosh – what used to be called a blackjack in gangster novels. He felt the first blow on his face and was aware of the blood running down his cheek. He screamed at the sickening pain as his clavicle cracked with the second blow. He heard the sirens as he fell, grasping at the car, and saw four policemen surrounding the two men by the Range Rover.

He wasn't unconscious for long. When he came around, Brockie was holding him and the whole car park was an arena of din: sirens wailing, tasers hissing, men shouting and a shot. Was it a shot? Bingham wasn't sure. He heard much running and struggling. A paramedic appeared, smiling, and leaned over him. The pain was too much. Before he passed out for the second time, he heard Brockie say:

"Well done, old man," said Brockie, "You've flushed the buggers out. We can leave the paperwork to the boys in blue."

Bingham sat at the kitchen table, his arm in a sling, the two terriers – Ben and George – on his lap with Pippa, the Labrador, trying to nose them off. The cats were under the kitchen table, ignoring him. Lina had just served him fish in the Milanese style, and he was washing it down with a glass of dry Orvieto. He was home and more than pleased to be there.

Seeing his injuries for the first time since he'd arrived in Britain (he'd phoned her but not gone home before dealing with Stefanich), Lina had been annoyed – much as she used to be when one of the children fell off the roof of an outhouse – but soon calmed down and spoiled him. While she cooked, she'd softly sung several of her favourite arias including one of Puccini's he loved 'O mio babbino caro'.

Bingham was feeling at peace. He'd made his statement; the NCIS officers had come to Bob's Farm. And what he considered to be the worst part of his ordeal was over: he'd been to see the family of Colin and Patty Mayhew. Lina had gone with him, driving them both to Lancashire where the children and their families lived. They'd stayed for several days and Lina had been a great help: listening, consoling and trying to understand with the families. They'd promised to return for the funeral, but now had time to themselves.

The cuts and bruises were healing. His doctor had looked him over and complimented the Spanish medics on their care and skill. He'd examined the results of the coshing: the laceration to the head and the broken clavicle. The wounds were a reminder of another world, a world where decent people like Lina and himself were not left alone to live their lives as they wished.

"Michael Crawford is starring in a musical version of *The Go-Between*, Bing," said Lina, suddenly breaking into his thoughts. "It's on at the Apollo Theatre. We could catch the train down from Ipswich and the journey on the underground is only a short one. I'm sure Phil will keep an eye on the animals."

"You've already bought the tickets, haven't you?"

"I thought it would be a nice break. You played old Leo in the non-musical version earlier this year."

Bingham smiled at his wife. She was bringing life back to normal. It had to be that way, or one would go insane. He also smiled to himself, knowing Lina would have realised that the play's very title had a certain, if unfortunate, aptness.

Spring 2016

ACKNOWLEDGEMENTS

Although this story is a fiction, its key events and descriptions are based on actual incidents and the experiences of people involved in similar situations and circumstances. Anyone wishing to delve deeper into the real world from which this novel is drawn should read the two excellent books by the investigative journalist and true crime writer, Wensley Clarkson

Gang Wars on the Costa: John Blake Publishing 2009
Hash: Quercus 2013